ORC-WARD ENCOUNTERS

SAM HALL

Orc-ward Encounters

Orc-ward Encounters © Sam Hall 2021

All rights reserved. No part of this book may be used or reproduced in any manner whatsoever without written permission except for in the case of brief quotations for the use in critical articles or reviews.

Cover art and design by Gombar Cover Designs
Edited by Bookish Dreams Editing

The characters and events depicted in this book are fictitious. Any similarity to real persons, living or dead, is coincidental and not intended by the author.

❀ Created with Vellum

Author Note

This book is written in Australian English, which is a weird lovechild of British and American English. We tend to spell things the way the Brits do (expect a lot more u's), yet also use American slang and swear more than both combined.

While many people have gone over this book, trying to find all the typos and other mistakes, they just keep on popping up like bloody rabbits. If you spot one, don't report it to Amazon, drop me an email at the below address so I can fix the issue.

samhall.author@gmail.com

Chapter 1

When it was like this, nothing was wrong. When I was drawing, reading, lost in some creative enterprise, everything was A-OK. My brain, my body, they came together as one shining thing.

I'd always loved the way my pen felt when it rolled across the page. Right now, my focus was completely narrowed down to that thin black line I was drawing. Uni-ball roller pens, they glided across the paper's surface, and sometimes that was a difficult thing. They could be a little hard to control, overshooting the long curves I was making, because I was drawing her.

An alter ego of sorts maybe? She was all generous curves and sassy attitude as she appeared on the page again with a long sweep of hair, big fluttery eyes, and the body of an earth goddess. I rendered her well rounded bust line, hips, and thighs using my box of special shading markers, starting to make her really pop off the page until she looked almost ready to shoot me a cheeky wink. I drew and I coloured and I tweaked, feeling her become more and more real, until....

Knock, knock, knock.

My head jerked up, and at first, I just blinked. House, room, door, visitor, they were all concepts that came back to me slowly. I got to my feet as another noun was supplied—Hannah.

"Oh my god, Laila!" my best friend in the world said, laden down with bags and bags of stuff. She dumped them on the ground and then held her arms out to me. *Hug Hannah*, my instincts told me, so I did.

"Oh shit…" Just a little squeak from me, and then Han was holding me at arm's length, staring at me semi-sternly.

"You forgot, didn't you?" I just stared back, smiling sheepishly. "You got drawing or watching anime or reading, and you forgot."

"I was drawing this character for—"

"Laila, you promised!"

I smiled, then nodded. I had promised. For the first time in forever, I was going to go out clubbing with my best friend and she was going to make me into the best version of myself.

"C'mon then! Help me get all this shit inside and let's get started."

"Hannah, it's only six PM," I said.

"I know. I'm not sure we'll have enough time."

"OH MY GOD, LAILA," Hannah exclaimed. "Look at you!"

I didn't want to. The mirror and me, we weren't friends. I might spend my evenings drawing fantastical plus size women, but for some reason when I looked at my reflection, that wasn't what I saw. But Hannah had primped and powdered and styled me to within an inch of my life, so I needed to take a look for her sake. I took a deep breath in. Well, as much as I could with this kind of shapewear on, and then turned around.

I saw why Hannah was excited, because this, this was the best reflection I'd seen. She'd blown out my hair and used some kind of wonder product in it that gave it serious volume and bounce. My mousy brown locks had been transformed into loose, effortless waves. My skin was smoothed, looking almost airbrushed in ways I'd only ever been able to achieve with a drawing. Every blemish, every blotch, it was all gone and there was only this.

Eyes that shone with lids coated in shimmery golds, bronzes, and coppers, bringing out golden highlights in my eyes I'd never seen before. Lips full, painted with a matte muted red that outlined their shape and drew your eye. The shapewear smoothed over all my lumps and bumps, giving me a shape as close to my drawings as possible, but not quite…

I was taller than average, and my weight even more so. I had big tits—yay!—a big arse—a bitch to find jeans for—but with that came a big stomach and big thighs. I was eternally grateful for the plethora of more Rubenesque pop stars and models, celebrating a greater variety of female beauty, but it didn't help me. Whether due to industrial style corsets or just God-given luck, they were all wasp waisted hourglasses—the universal signifier of female attractiveness. But me? I wasn't an hourglass or even a pear. I was an apple.

"Polycystic ovary syndrome," my endocrinologist had said, peering over his glasses. "Women are usually exempt from the vagaries of testosterone. When you put on weight, it's on your hips or your buttocks and thighs. It creates less of a risk of heart disease, cancer… Unfortunately, due to your condition, you have higher levels of testosterone in your body. It causes the heavy periods you came to see me for and the problem with facial hair you're experiencing."

My hand had shot to my chin, a flare of shame washing through me. I'd thought I'd tweezed out the lot of the errant thick hairs that appeared on my chin, not wanting the doctor or the world to see them. He just nodded slowly.

"Weight loss will be incredibly difficult, but it's your only option. If you're to have any chance of having a child, you'll need to get your weight down. That way, you'll be able to avoid most of the worst effects of metabolic syndrome. I'll write you out a script for Metformin, but you'll need to…"

He faded away, but this remained, this whole other me. *Will it be enough?* I thought, furiously trying to hide my discomfort behind a smile. The tight dress, the heels, the makeup, the hair… Hannah had worked her magic to the best of her ability, and this was certainly the most attractive version of me possible, but… I let out a long sigh so slowly, I hoped she didn't notice.

This was the problem with us, the original odd couple. I wanted to hang back, stay in, lose myself in dreams and books and TV shows, but Hannah? She had that perfect blonde, doll-like beauty that should've made her a total alpha bitch, but was instead somehow an externalisation of the gorgeous girl inside. She thrived on music and dancing and hanging out with her throngs of adoring male fans until two AM. She was always willing to hang out with me here and watch endless marathons of movies with me, but now it was my turn…

"You did an amazing job, Hannah," I said, injecting all the sincerity I could into my voice. I was used to pretending. I did it all the time. "C'mon, let's call that Uber."

"Pre drinks first!" she said, throwing her arms up and then around me. "We need to get a head start because prices of cocktails at bars are crazy. C'mon, I'll whip you up some of my favourites."

As we walked downstairs, the frustration set in, triggered by the difficulty I had in performing such a small task in perilously high heels. Women all the way across the world did this every night. Going to clubs and dancing was some kind of feminine birthright I was heir to just as much as any other girl. It was the primitive mating ritual of our people, so why did it piss me off so much?

When I was drawing, my mind and my body knew what to do. I could drop down into a flow state that might last minutes or hours, and out it would all come. I'd look at my drawings afterward and see their flaws but also the beauty in them. But now? I was a fish out of water, gasping for breath, and I couldn't even acknowledge I was asphyxiating.

"I'm so glad you're doing this with me!" Hannah said, opening her bags, pulling out bottles and other concoctions with frightening speed. She pulled out her blender and some cocktail glasses and then showed off her skills as a mixologist. "You're going to have an amazing time! The club we're going to, Ingress—"

"Like the game?" I asked.

"What?"

"There's a game, it's what *Pokémon Go* was…" My voice trailed away. "It doesn't matter," I said finally.

"Well, this Ingress has amazing drinks. I don't even know what's in them sometimes, but the barmen are fiiine. The music's great and it's always packed, but I manage to get in each time."

Well, no surprise there. Hannah had a kind of beauty that was almost otherworldly. Like if a pair of jewel encrusted wings appeared from between her shoulder blades, I wouldn't have been surprised. In ancient times, they would have worshipped her as a demi goddess or something, but right now, she was just my friend.

"You know, you might meet someone there."

Her voice became coy, her eyes studiously making sure she was pouring the right amount of alcohol into the blender to make the next lot of drinks.

"Someone nice. Someone who sees what I see…"

I had never envied Hannah her beauty. She had dickheads and creepers dogging her steps every time she went out. She worked as a fashion buyer, and men frequently thought they had a right to her time when she was busy at work or waiting in the line at the shops, all because there was something about the amazing symmetry of her face. It inspired desire in them, and that needed to be seen to, now, irrespective of what she thought about it.

But I did envy her one thing.

The boyfriends she'd had fell for her, hard. I'd literally had to talk one of them off the roof of her apartment building when they broke up. They loved her with a depth, a passion, a heat I could only marvel at. That, I wanted that more than anything.

"Maybe," I replied, noncommittally.

"Well, drink up!" she said, and I did, lifting the ice blue drink to my lips, pleasantly surprised by the rush of citrus the colour did not indicate at all. My eyes widened, and I blinked. Sweet, sour, cold, mint, and something else… "Good? I knew you'd like my potions! Let's have another couple while we wait for the Uber."

She pressed the button on the blender and then grabbed her phone, opening the app, wrinkling her nose when she saw the wait for a ride.

"More than a couple, it looks like," she said. "I should've pre-scheduled. Oh well!" She grinned at me, then took my glass before drinking down her own. The blender was stopped and another concoction was produced, poured into the glass like a lemon slushy, but this one had a salted rim. "Margaritas…" Hannah said, pushing the glass over to me, then turning on my stereo. She threw her arms up in the air, shimmying her hips before sweeping her drink up and taking a sip.

"Dance with me," she said, faking a sultry tone.

"No, no, no…" I tried to back away from her and stumbled. "Hannah, I agreed to come out with you."

"Come dancing," she corrected.

"Nope, that wasn't what I said. Someone needs to keep an eye on your handbag as you bump and grind. That's my job. Wingman." I ticked off one finger. "Bag minder." I ticked off another. "Drink schlepper." That last bit came out a bit spitty, like my tongue was just a little too big for my mouth. "Waiter. Drink waiter."

"You're not going to be my waiter," she admonished. "You're my friend, my best friend." She stopped her snake-like moves, grabbing my hands in hers and holding them for a second. "You've been there for me through everything, and I can't say that about many people. You'd still be there for me if I was in a horrible car accident tomorrow and I lost 'the face.'" She waved her hand across her features in a dismissive way. Sometimes I wondered if it was more burden than blessing, particularly when she talked about her beauty in almost third person. "It's me and you forever, babe. Chicks before dicks."

Which was how I came to be wedged into the back of a

small hatchback, driving across town to Hannah's favourite club as the Uber driver did his level best to impress my friend. She kept trying to include me in the conversation, but I resisted and, bluntly, so did he. *Camouflage*, I thought. *Blend in, fade away.*

And so, I did.

Chapter 2

I was a bit pissed.

Now if you're an American, you'll be thinking that means I'm angry, and that wasn't it at all. The alcohol had hit my system, leaving me floating free and in my own head, the bright lights and throbbing sounds of the club a blaring background. No, in Australia, it means drunk.

Get pissed, getting on the piss, being a piss pot, piss weak. For some reason, we were very, very focussed on urine, and why was that? Also bugger, a term for anal intercourse, historically seen to being between two men. We peppered our conversations with it like that Salt Bae meme. There was even a national car ad that had used the term when I was a little kid. So…where was I? Oh, yeah, the club.

"C'mon!" Hannah said, linking her arm with mine and hauling me along, resulting in something I was sure resembled a giraffe in roller skates, legs going everywhere, shaking, shaking, ankles twitching as I sought to get them under control and follow Hannah up to the door. People were lined up, but she didn't care. She didn't need to. The velvet rope used to cordon off the entrance was unclipped, but the burly bouncer's hand hesitated when he saw me.

"She's with you?"

"Yep. Laila's my bestest friend in the whoole world."

OK, so Hannah was pissed too.

"Sure," the man said with a shrug, letting us in, much to the disgruntlement of the people in line. I heard some shitty comments, felt hot eyes stabbing into my body as we walked on through, but being pissed was awesome. I passed by, not even sparing them a look, and whatever they said seemed to slide off my now Teflon coated skin.

"Let's get a drink," I said as we entered the dark bowels of the club.

"Yass, bitch!" Hannah squealed, hungry eyes turning our way, taking my friend in, assessing her, then readying their approach, but not yet. I needed alcohol, lots of alcohol, if I was to serve as a good wingman tonight, and that was what we'd do.

"Drinks, my good man," I said, throwing myself at the bar, a space having cleared itself the moment we arrived. I'd seen lots of people waiting to be served, so that was weird, but hey, we were here. A barman's eyes jerked up, meeting mine, and whoa, whoa, whoa. Bar staff were not allowed to look that hot. He smiled the smug bastard smile of the truly stunning and then asked for our order.

"And what can I get you two fair maidens?"

"Lime margaritas, Clayton," Hannah said, reaching for her purse. "A jug if you will."

"No need for that," Clayton said with a shake of his head, grabbing a blender and loading it up with ice, juice, and alcohol. "The gents over there have volunteered to buy you a drink."

We peered down the glossy black bar and saw a cluster of very, very good-looking men standing there. Hannah's teeth sank into her bottom lip, her tell when she was attracted to someone, or in this case, someones, but she shook her head, turning back to Clayton.

"Nope, I'm good. I'll pay for this—"

"Hannah…" I said.

"It's fine. If I accept their offer, they'll think… Well, they'll think stuff, and that's not what tonight's about." She turned to me, smiling bright. "I'm going to show you that life's not just chillaxing in front of Netflix. It can be dancing and drinking too."

"There you go, princess," the barman said. Obviously, he knew Hannah well if he was calling her that. The jug of frosty margaritas was set on the bar, as well as two salt encrusted glasses, but when she went to pay, the dudes appeared.

"We can't have a beautiful woman like yourself paying for your own drinks," a tall man with meticulously cut hair said. It'd been clipped short at the sides, then styled to sweep over to the left. His sharp green eyes bore into Hannah's, a small smile forming. "I'm Leonard, and these are my friends."

"And this is my friend, Laila."

Oh no. Oh god no. I shouldn't have thought that. I had as much a right as anyone to be drinking at a club. I was a human being, a smart, caring, awesome human being, but as soon as the collective eyes of the pack of free ranging Abercrombie and Fitch models turned my way, I pressed myself back against the bar and this was why.

You're going to think I have a self-esteem problem and maybe I do, but I don't think it actually comes from thinking I'm shit. I know I'm not, but as soon as I felt their cool gazes on me, sizing me up and dismissing me with no more thought than one would a wilted head of lettuce at Woolies, the temptation was to feel like I was shit. They called these places the meat market for a reason, because we were all commodities, and people like Hannah were rare and valuable ones and people like me weren't.

My heart raced faster and faster, my breath shallow and rapid, so that when the pack of really, really, really, ridiculously good-looking dudes turned away, I let out a gusty sigh of relief. Hannah and the guys were involved in a flirty little argument about who should pay, though I was pretty sure she would win. She'd stick by me—that was what they didn't get and that was

Orc-ward Encounters

why she was my best friend. I turned back to the barman, who was just waiting patiently for this to resolve, ignoring the growing line of customers.

"Look, I really need a drink if I'm going to sit through this," I said, my drunken haze starting to lift. "I'll pay for these."

The man just stared for a moment, but it wasn't a harsh thing. It was like he was…searching or something, then finally, he nodded. He straightened up, pulling down a glass and scooping ice into it, his hands moving in a blur as he added ingredients into a cocktail shaker. He shot me a sardonic smile, his eyes flicking to Hannah and her harem before he cracked the shaker over the top of the glass and then put the drink before me. It was a very lurid bright green, but something about the spicy scent of it drew me closer.

"Whoa, what's that?" I asked. "I'll just pay for—"

"Take it," he said with a shrug.

I frowned slightly, not sure what the implication was here.

"Well, how much do I owe you?" I asked.

"On the house," he said with a shrug. "You'll need it, dealing with those dickheads."

And before I could protest, he turned to the barman next to him, explained the kerfuffle with paying for the margaritas and then turned and left, the exasperated cries of the waiting customers completely ignored.

"Look, mate, let the lady pay for her bloody drinks," the replacement barman said to the pretty boys. "If you have to argue this hard, she's not fucking interested."

I'd taken a big sip of the green drink, the result this rich, cinnamon, apple thing that kinda tasted like an apple pie had had a bottle of whiskey drizzled all over it, but when I heard the barman bawl the guy out, I snorted, feeling it rush up to my nose. I blinked and swallowed furiously, trying to dispel the fizzy sensation.

"Right, well, you should've just said," chief dude bro said in a huff.

"I fucking did, multiple times." I stared at Hannah, her voice pure ice right now. You didn't see it often, but when you did… She stood as tall as her diminutive height allowed, fairly bristling with anger. Uh-oh, the pretty boys had screwed up big time. She slapped her card down on the bar and said, "I want to pay for my drinks and get out of your way."

"Oh thank goddd…" someone in line said.

The barman nodded and then put the transaction through, passing Hannah her card back, and she scooped up the jug and the glass with expert ease, dragging me away from the bar. As I turned around, it was me that got the stink eye from the dude bros, which was why I hated coming to this kind of place. I drank the rest of the green drink down, depositing the empty glass on a table as we passed, the people there turning around in irritation, but I paid them no mind. I couldn't, or I'd go scuttling out the door and home. No matter what I was out in the real world, here I was reduced down to the fat friend.

Look that up on Urban Dictionary if you don't believe me. Men have decided to record for posterity on the internet the 'obstacle' we present in them getting to the girl they actually want. I staggered after my friend, taking a seat at a table that miraculously had become vacant as Hannah worked on the drinks.

"Sorry about before. Those guys were dicks."

Were they?

"The margaritas here are freaking delish. Try one."

She pushed a glass towards me, and as my hands wrapped around the glass, the feeling of not only being a fish out of water, but a fish who'd been dumped in a vat of hydrochloric acid with mutant sharks swimming around, hit me.

"We'll have a few drinks," she said, looking at the jug. "Then we'll have a dance." She swayed in her seat. "It'll be amazing."

As I stared at the dance floor, watching people move with a kind of grace that made my heart hurt, I could see why she would think so. There were people of all sizes there too, something I forced myself to notice. I wanted to believe this was a place only for gym bunnies and bros, but there was a lot greater variety here than I'd thought there would be, so for a moment, I just watched them move hypnotically.

"All right," I said, agreeing with Hannah belatedly. "Let's do that."

"Well, cheers, big ears!" she said, clinking her glass with mine.

Chapter 3

I'd just ducked out to the loo for a brief moment, but by the time I arrived back, they were there. Two men this time, different ones, but to paraphrase Jane Austen, it is a truth universally acknowledged, that a woman on her own in possession of a beautiful visage, must be in want of male attention. Hannah was chatting to the guys as she waited, but she kept her distance. One, with tawny brown hair and a crisp white shirt open at the neck, kept trying to lean in and brush his fingers against hers, but her body language was very contained.

"Here she is!" Hannah said, her face lighting up when she caught sight of me. The two men turned to see what was causing all this excitement and took me in. Their gazes were cool, objective, no smiles coming my way, but no outright revulsion. Yeah, I could work my wingman magic here. Hannah wouldn't say so, but she'd told me enough times about what she got up to at clubs to know how this would go. She came, she drank, she partied, and then she had crazy monkey sex with hot dudes. Tonight, she was willing to forgo all of that to try and share with me the fun of going clubbing. Well, not on my watch. I grabbed my drink, taking a long sip.

"Hey, I'm Laila."

I used the same cool, professional tone I brought out during job interviews or when talking to my landlord, which for some reason, seemed to settle the guys.

"Hi, Laila," the guy who wasn't edging closer to Hannah said. "I'm Greg, and this is River."

"Hi," River said, barely sparing me a glance, his smile spreading slowly as he gazed at Hannah.

"Well, it's lovely to meet you, but my friend and I are here to dance so—"

"Actually, I kinda twisted my ankle on the way back from the loos," I said, sitting down on the barstool abruptly. "I'll be OK. I just need to rest it for a bit."

River's smile became brilliant at that, the golden light transforming my friend's face. He held out a hand and said, "If you want to dance?"

She eyed his hand suspiciously, then shook her head. "I should—"

"Go," I said. "You should go. You shouldn't miss out on a good night because I'm a clumsy dickhead. Go, go."

I shooed her away with my hand, something that just made her giggle, not feeling like I could relax until she took River's hand and he led her out onto the dance floor.

"Well, that was very…selfless of you," Greg said. "You didn't twist your ankle, did you?"

"Nope, and if I'm guessing correctly, your mate River has asked you to stay here and keep me sweet so he's got a clear shot with Hannah," I said drily, watching the two of them dance.

River was very good, moving around her like some kind of snake. Graceful, deadly, but there was a beauty to that. I took another sip of my drink, the acidic burn feeling just right. Greg snorted in response to my comment.

"Not in so many words, but yeah, that's the bro code."

"Well, the sister code is this." I turned to face him, taking in his high cheekbones and full lips. "If River's Mr Right or Mr Right Now for Hannah, then I'm not going to get in her way.

She's like a sister to me, literally. I want her to be happy, and if he can give her that for however long she allows, I'm cool. So we don't need to do…this." I waved my hand around vaguely.

Greg let out a short bark of a laugh.

"And what is this?" he asked, copying my hand wave.

"Pretend like you're here for anything other than to help your mate get laid. Fuck, if there's someone here you want to chase, go and do so. Honestly, I just want to go home and curl up in my bed and take a few aspirin and drink a big bottle of water, but I promised Hannah I'd come out with her."

"You sound…sad."

"I guess I am," I said. "She's my best friend, has been for so long, and this is her element, not mine."

I straightened up, looked around me, seeing the club as if for the first time. I didn't like to dance, I never had. I'd always listened to heavy metal and rock music, which Hannah said was nigh undanceable to. I liked to read and draw, and she hated that, getting bored even when watching TV, let alone requiring herself to focus for long periods of time. We had very little common ground, and for some reason, that hit me right now, hard. She was the person I was closest to in the world, and yet…

"And what is your element, Laila?" Greg asked, a kind of low-key amusement in his expression.

So I told him, because I'd warned him away and he'd stayed. We both knew what we were doing—placating our friends, allowing them to have fun on the dance floor, thinking we were OK. I talked about comics and the zines I drew and some of my favourite fandoms like it was perfectly fine to do so, because bloody hell, right now it was. Greg nodded along and asked relevant questions until I turned the focus back to him.

He told me about the outdoor adventure company he and River ran and some of the crazy places they'd taken groups of customers too. He regaled me with stories about some of the worst. High-maintenance Karens refusing to follow safety protocols and arguing until they'd been forced to refund their money, just so they would go away. Weekend warriors who wanted to prove they could still go hard, then ended up having to be carried back on a bush walk. We chatted until Hannah came rushing back, cheeks flushed.

"Well, you two have been talking for a while," she said in a suggestive tone that made my blood run cold. *Don't put me in this position*, I thought furiously. *Don't.*

"Yeah, we've been talking a little about the new Batman adaption that's coming out," I replied. She stiffened at that. Both of us had nominated keywords that indicated we weren't interested, so guys could be moved on. Batman was my keyword. "But I think you're going to really like R-Patz as the Dark Knight."

Hannah worked out the subtext easily enough, even if River just looked confused. When she shot him a sidelong look, a speculative one, as if to assess if she wanted to keep him around, he settled instantly.

"Come and dance with me," she said to me, smiling brightly. "You promised…"

I had, hadn't I? So why was I slipping off my stool and edging away?

"I've gotta go to the loo."

Hannah's face fell at that, her brow creasing. We were back in the place we always were, pulling in two different directions. I'd said I'd try but… My eyes darted around the club, the sounds, the clothes, the alcohol… My skin felt like it was burning hot, discomfort an actual physical sensation.

"I'll be back and then—" I tried to explain.

"Come on," River said, taking Hannah's arm and tugging her after him, letting me make a clean getaway.

My heels wobbled, my thighs shaking as I stalked over to the toilets, head down. People rarely came to clubs alone. Somehow, the space didn't allow for that, and when you were, you felt vulnerable, like some weak old caribou at the edge of the herd. I shoved the toilet door in, thankful it was largely empty, and found a stall.

"Laila?" I heard Hannah call out moments later. "Laila?"

"In here," I replied. "Won't be long."

"Hey, if you're not having fun, we can go home, y'know. I'm grateful you came and…"

But that would mean curtailing her fun, and I couldn't bring myself to do that.

"Nah, I'm fine. I'll be out soon."

"OK, well, I'll see you back at the table."

I waited some minutes, then finished what I was doing, sure if I left it long enough, she'd be on the dance floor with River or whoever Mr Right Now ended up being. When I came out, I went to the sinks and washed my hands, then looked up.

It felt like I was staring at a mask of someone else's face, bleached pale by the artificial lights, the makeup underlining and overemphasising things until it didn't look like it was my face at all, so I just blinked and jerked my eyes away. I stumbled outside, the haze of alcohol well and truly kicking in now, before zeroing in on the table.

It was empty, Hannah having gone to dance, and the guys had gone where?

"I thought you were going to seal the deal with the fat one," a masculine voice hissed, and somehow, out of all the noise in this place, that was what I caught. Other women my size didn't have this issue, didn't seem to be uniquely sensitised to the opinions of dickheads. They either sailed past, oblivious, or didn't give a fucking shit, but not me. Part of me seemed to almost seek it out, these poisonous words, and I could never work out why.

"There was no deal to seal. She knew the drill and was quite blunt about it. She bullshitted on about comics or some geeky shit, but she said straight up, nothing was going to happen, but she wasn't going to get in the way of you and Hannah. It was kinda sweet in a way."

"Sweet? The pretty friend is never going to ditch the ugly one. I needed you to put the moves on. I took one for the team the other night with that fugly bitch…"

I don't know why I reacted the way I did. It was harsh and cruel, but I didn't even know these idiots. Their opinion meant next to nothing to me, and yet I jerked back as if slapped. Maybe because alcohol was doing the thinking, not my brain. Maybe because I'd felt so helplessly bloody awkward since the moment I started getting dressed. This wasn't me, my soul had cried out the whole time, and still I'd forced myself to do this. Well, not anymore.

I changed course drastically, striding towards the door, but there were people, so many people in the way. I stumbled into some, pushed past others, more abuse ringing in my ears, but I shoved that to one side as I did them. Some shouts, some cries, and then I was out.

"You right there, mate?" the doorman asked me, looking me up and down with a frown.

"Fine," I snapped back, taking off my heels and carrying them. Fuck. Yes. Then I closed my eyes for a second, feeling the breeze on my face, the cool of the night air settling me in ways nothing else had.

"What the fuck is up with her?" someone asked, cutting through the calm.

That was what triggered me—some random question from a person I couldn't even put a face to. I turned tail and ran, wanting, needing to get away. That pulsed in my blood over and over, *go, go, go*. I stumbled, staggered, then righted myself, veering across the road when a group of men started walking up the footpath towards me, hearing a car horn before I floundered off the road and into a nearby park. Not the right place for a woman to be in the middle of the night, but whatever devil had me in its grip, this made perfect sense. I felt the grass under my feet, the cool dew, and…

Before it happened, I heard the sounds of drums, which made me assume it was just another club with either live music or a DJ playing, but that wasn't it. The sounds were much more primal, rising and rising, blocking out all others. I looked up and saw the moon glowing bright, so bright, and squinted, as it seemed so much bigger. I stepped forward, into the gloom of the park, the benches and play equipment shadowy shapes under the moonlight, but that wasn't where I was going. It was the place between.

That was the last real thought I had before it happened. *The place between.* What the hell did that mean? I'd ask myself that a lot later, but right now, I stepped from the dark into the darker, a strange, velvety blackness swallowing me up…

Then spitting me out.

When I looked around me, the park wasn't there anymore, no more drums, no more anything. Just trees, the sleepy calls of birds, and the three moons.

Wait, what?

I blinked, staring up at the night sky, seeing the lambent circles of cool white light at different places in the darkness, unable to look away from the sight of something no human had seen, which was perhaps how I missed them. I stumbled over a tree root and went flying into a bush that seemed to want to get to know me much more intimately, the branches tearing at my clothes and my hair. I finally pulled myself free, flying forward and landing on the ground in front of them.

Three pairs of bare feet, broad, well made, but fucking huge. And green. Did I mention green? Not the bright acid green of my drink, but a flat kind of olive drab. I just stared, seeing in perfect detail where each man had filed his toenails straight, where one had a snaking scar that led from the top of his foot up to his ankle. I followed it up, up, up until I saw the three of them standing there.

"Holy fucking shit," I exclaimed, gasping. "It's the Incredible Hulk times three!"

Chapter 4

"Um…hi," I said to what were undoubtedly figments of my imagination. Even if they were imaginary, it paid to be polite. They were kinda fuzzy from where I was sitting, on the ground at their feet, but that problem was soon resolved. Massive hands reached for me, and I tried to scramble away, but I was picked up like I was nothing and tucked into a very broad chest—a very nice, very muscular, still olive green chest.

"A human woman," one man said, taking in a long breath.

"What is a human doing out here in the woods at night? They know these are our lands." A pensive pause. "But she smells so sweet."

"Sweet indeed," the man holding me said. "Sweet enough to draw others into our territory. We must make haste and return to the cave."

"Cave, haste, smell…?" I blinked, trying to get my alcohol blurred vision to clear, but I was stunned when I did.

They had very nice eyes, each one of them. Large and dark, glittering in the moonlight, or moons' light, they had those kinds of thick lashes boys are always blessed with and girls resort to falsies to imitate. Each one had a strong, proud face, the face of a warrior, though where had that idea come from? What the hell did I know of warriors? Nothing, but if I did, I'd expect them to look like this.

The one holding me had a broad face, with two whorling scars that had been carved into the tops of his cheekbones and a powerful jaw that my fingers itched to trace the line of. The face of the one on the left was thinner, more angular, his brows seeming permanently pulled down, with sharp angular scars marking the harsh hollows of his cheeks, but the last one? His eyes twinkled as he stared at me. He was the only one with shorter hair, a shock of black hair that looked like it had been ruffled often, and as if to prove my theory, he raised his hand, raking it through it.

But all of this is skirting around what I was really staring at. It was their tusks. Yup, read that again—tusks. Sharp white fangs that protruded past the edges of their bottom lips, curling up over their top one. Oh, and the olive green skin. I stared and stared, the amused one's smile only widening as my eyes darted from one to the other. I knew what this was, who these guys were, I just had to—

"Orcs!" I said, letting out a gusty sigh, but the relief of finding the word was quickly lost. "Orcs…?"

"Yes, we are—"

"Cosplay?" I said to myself, all the men's brows jerking down now. "You're orc cosplayers hanging around in a park in the middle of night outside… Shit." I began to wriggle now. I needed to get down, get away, get my phone, and—

"Peace, woman," the orc—no, the cosplayer holding me hissed.

His eyes and those of his mates scanned the surroundings, and holy fucking shit, Batman! The other two retrieved these fuck-off big machete type things from sheaths strapped across their backs, but there was no weird scraping sound you heard in movies. Then the two men dropped down into loose crouches, moving forward on catlike feet.

"I'll get the woman to the cave," the cosplayer holding me

said in a harsh whisper, and wasn't that as ominous as shit? "You remove any that would dare trespass on our territory."

"Cave?" My voice was starting to rise, my pulse beginning to race, my muscles tensing to fight my way free of this admittedly really fucking strong man's grip, when a hand slapped across my mouth, silencing me very effectively.

"Not until we are safe, my lovely."

And that was when I knew I'd fallen and hit my head somehow. I was slowly bleeding to death of some subdural haematoma or whatever they talked about in medical dramas. It was either that or I was tripping fucking balls on something someone had slipped into my drink.

Which strangely reminded me of that bright green cocktail the mysterious barman had poured for me.

But I didn't get to ponder the implications of drink spiking because we were on the move. For a big guy—actually, make that a massive guy, he could move like a goddamn panther, slipping through trees and bushes while barely making a sound, carrying me like I was no more than a kitten, refusing to stop when the sounds of weapons clashing cut through the air. If anything, he moved faster, making my head spin nauseatingly. My stomach felt like it was bouncing along with his every stride, jostling and swirling as he broke out into a run, but right as I was about to claw at this slightly kidnappy cosplayer's arm to let me down so I could vomit all that expensive alcohol in the bushes, he came to a stop.

"And what do we have here, young Vargan?"

The voice dripped pure malice, something that quelled my nausea and replaced it with fear. That didn't improve when I caught a look at the speaker. If the guys that had found me looked like a bunch of rugby players cosplaying as their *Warcraft* avatars, this guy looked like something from a Peter Jackson wet dream. Because this guy? Imagine that The Incredible Hulk had fucked a mountain and nine months later, a bouncing baby rock formation was born, complete with craggy features, boulder-like muscles, and brutal fangs that had been chipped and broken in battle. Badass. He was a scary, motherfucking badass.

"Stay behind me," my dude, Vargan, said, setting me carefully down on my feet. He pulled the biggest fucking blade off his back, one that made Cloud from *Final Fantasy VII's* look like a cheese knife. "We found the woman, Urzog. By our laws, we have the right of first courting—"

"Courting, pah!" Urzog, the man-slash-mountain spat a great big loogie out on the ground. Gross. "Women are for the taking, not for soft things like that." He drew his own weapon then, the moons' light shining off the steely surface. "I follow my ways. I take what I want, and you won't be the one to stop me."

"No?" The cosplayer with the thinner face walked out of the tree line, the short-haired one in tow. I noted the smears of blood on their blades and across their cheeks, and that was when shit got real for me. I looked at Urzog, Vargan and them, and some other explanation for my predicament came to me. I stared up at those three moons, those totally unable to be cosplayed moons, and had a small epiphany. My throat was suddenly bone-dry and too thick to swallow.

These were orcs.

Orcs who were about to fight.

Orcs who were dragging me off to their cave.

Another orc who wanted to…

I couldn't think anymore, my chill well and truly deserting me as I jerked away from Vargan and went running off into the darkness…

Except I barely got five steps away when the short-haired guy grabbed me, holding me close to his body.

"Shh…" he said in a low voice. "All will be well. Urzog is the devil on the battlefield, but Vargan?"

"Vargan would climb into the bowels of hell and tear the devil asunder if it meant protecting a woman," the orc with the thinner face said. "And so will we. I am Kren, and this is Ghain. Who might you be?"

"Laila," I said, my mouth hanging open. "I'm Laila."

Kren nodded. "A beautiful name, Lay-la, but I must ask you to stay put as we teach this overblown windbag the error of coming into our territory."

Ghain stroked his hand through my hair, and then the two of them moved as one, drawing their weapons and going to stand beside Vargan.

"Enough talk. The Mothers witness this affront and will decide the outcome," Vargan said, the words taking on a ceremonial slant. "Raise your weapon and declare your intent, or walk away."

Urzog spat on the ground again—apparently, he was big on that—and did just as they said, lifting a massive cleaver of a weapon. He smiled as my eyes went wide at the sheer size of it. *If it landed, it would shear these orcs' arms off at the joint*, I thought. Urzog seemed to think the same, again grinning madly as he swept the blade in a huge arc. I could only stare as it cut through the air, all the power in those boulder-like arms giving it the kind of momentum that seemed to slice down and towards...

Not the guys. Their weapons were much smaller, but they allowed them to be much more nimble. They were up and under the blade's sweep, slashing out at Urzog, the massive orc bellowing as each found their mark. Just little glancing cuts right now, it appeared they were playing with their food, just like cats, and Urzog responded as if they were. He roared at them like a maddened beast, his eyes seeming to flash red in the moons' light.

"Cowards! You fight like humans, with little pricking blows. Face me like a true son of Golag of the Blood!"

"You came onto our territory," Ghain said with a grin. "We can face a challenger in any way we wish."

"If our weapons are so puny, then you will surely best us," Kren added mildly.

"Enough playing. Come forth and prove yourself, or begone from our lands." Vargan looked back over his shoulder at me. "We have far pleasanter company to entertain."

"I'll tear the little bitch in two, just to hear her scream,"

Urzog snarled, and then without warning, he launched himself at the three orcs.

This was supposed to be some sort of surprise attack, I thought. Like, I'd watched plenty of sword play in movies, because helllo, *The Witcher*. Urzog seemed to rely heavily on his mass and his huge arse sword to do the work for him, so the three orcs were moving, striking out at their opponent as he passed in a way that seemed almost wolf-like. There were no theatrics, no big displays or guttural roars of intimidation, they were in and dancing away with a kind of balletic grace that, I had to admit, yanked me entirely out of my existential spiral of dread and forced me to acknowledge the moment.

They worked with deadly precision, beating back and blocking all of Urzog's attacks and countering with devastating ones of their own, and together, they worked in a way that had to have come from long years of practice. They moved with such grace my mouth fell open. Then finally, Urzog was brought to his knees by a series of devastating slashes to the backs of his thighs. The massive orc had already been tiring, but those last few strikes stripped him of the last of his reserves. Vargan moved forward, his axe-sword-thingy held out and laid across the back of Urzog's neck, a feeling of dread rising in me.

"You have been found wanting by the Mothers," he said in a quietly confident tone. "Your challenge has failed. Do you withdraw or do you wish to suffer the Mothers' wrath?"

For a moment, the only sound was Urzog sucking in breaths, but finally, he answered.

"I withdraw."

"By our laws, if you come into our territory without our permission again, your life is forfeit. All orckind will turn their hearts against you, their arms will become ours, to mete out the Mothers' justice. Do you accept this judgement?"

"I do."

"The rest of your band is back there in the forest," Kren said. "Remove this stain from our lands and do not return. Your judgement is theirs."

"My judgement is theirs."

It was weird to see such a massive orc get to his feet, looking as surly as a spanked child, but there we were. Just as they said, he disappeared back into the forest, no doubt to collect his mates. Though with the immediate danger gone, came the other threat. The three of them turned to me. Vargan pushed his long black plaits back over his shoulder, the span of his bare shoulders and broad chest clear in the moons' light. He was powerful, which was why he'd been able to pick me up with such ease. He had to be at least seven feet tall, maybe taller, and the others were about the same. Kren had his plaits bound back with a strip of leather, but the sides of his head were shaved clean, emphasising the lean structure of his face. And Ghain? He just grinned, a wild light in his eyes.

"Woman," Vargan said, eyeing me now.

"Lay-la," Kren corrected. "Daughter of…?"

"Tracey," I supplied on automatic. "My mum's name is Tracey."

"Lay-la, daughter of Tray-cee," Vargan said. "My band and I claim the right of first courting."

"Um…what?" I asked, my head twisting as a feeling of utter incredulity washed over me. "What the hell is first courting when it's at home?"

He frowned slightly at that, because apparently, that wasn't the right answer.

"You came onto orc lands unmated," Ghain said in confusion. "Surely you knew what that meant?"

"No, no, see, I was trying to tell you." My eyes jerked up, drawn to those moons again. "This isn't my world. I didn't know these were orc lands. I don't know what first courting is, and I don't know why Urzog the man mountain was willing to fight you for that. No. No."

The three men frowned, then looked at each other, a quick discussion had before they turned back to me.

"However you came to be in our territory, any human

woman found in the orc lands may be claimed by our people," Vargan said. "You are…free to go, but—"

"But you are just as likely to run into Urzog or an orc of his ilk," Ghain said unhappily. "Come with us to our cave. At the very least, you'll be safe."

This earned him a sharp hiss from the other two, but he just shrugged, and for some reason, that sold me on the idea. I was tired, still drunk, spinning in a little globe of unreality as my mind fought to accept the unacceptable. A cave sounded just dandy right about now.

"Sure," I said, right as a wash of something cold and white passed through me, my knees giving out as I fell to the ground. Then there was only darkness as something that smelled so good surrounded me.

Chapter 5

"We need to get Judith here."

"Wash her face. It's what my mother always told me to do. I never worked out why."

"Because it cleanses the remains of your dinner off it and stops you stinking like offal. Perhaps it was that smell that had her swooning. I'm getting some cloths and soaking them in water. My mother always put them on her wrists when she was ill."

"To what purpose? Humans are strange."

"Who knows the mysteries of women? We don't."

"No, we don't."

"Then we need to get the…"

I blinked, then blinked again, hoping as soon as I was conscious that I would open my eyes to stare at my bedroom ceiling, that this had all been a drunken delusion. Instead, I saw wisps of wood smoke, creating a haze inside the cave, and them. Three massive green orcs.

"Ah, H—"

My throat instantly seized as I tried to speak, so I was hauled upright, a massive hand patting me on my back, my whole body shaking with the impact, as a horn brimming full of water was thrust at me. *Ghain*, my brain sluggishly supplied. The short-haired orc was Ghain. I took the water gratefully, sucking it down, even if drinking from what looked like a highly polished cow horn seemed a little *Conan the Barbarian*, but beggars couldn't be choosers in this scenario. They all hunched closer, creating a massive wall of man flesh between the mouth of the cave and me. They took in the way I drank the water down with greedy eyes, seeming to need to watch every moment, and then when I'd drained it, Ghain got to his feet to get a refill.

"I'll fill the horn," Kren said, reaching out to take the cup.

He had long, powerful fingers, and on the end of each one were sharp black nails, their composition much thicker than my flimsy things. He froze when I took in those vicious-looking talons, but then pressed ahead, gently taking the horn from me. I heard him step away but didn't see much as the other two shifted in.

"You are well, Lay-la?" Vargan asked, his concern apparent in his frown.

"Well?" I looked around me at the orcs, this cave, the furniture they had obviously created, and the weapons stacked against the wall. "I…"

"Don't press the woman," Kren said, returning with the horn and handing it over. I took another sip, the cold, slightly mineral tasting water helping to ground me. "We need cushions."

Ghain got to his feet, retrieving several stuffed animal skins, moving to prop them up behind me, then dropping down to offer a tanned fur. It was soft, thick, and had a grey flecked pelt.

"You must keep warm, Lay-la," he said. All three of them seemed to struggle to get their mouth around my name. "You are not orc. You will catch a chill."

My brow creased at that. It was such a mumsy thing to say, but somehow, it was charming, even if coming from a seven-foot-tall jolly green giant. Giant… Up close, I could see it all—the ways our faces were different. The orcs were bigger, their bones seeming thicker and heavier. There was nothing soft in Ghain's face at all, except for his expression. He stared at me as I stared back, fighting to accept what was in front of me. My hand jerked up, Ghain assuming it was to take the fur, but that wasn't it. *Please be cosplay*, I said over and over in my head. *Please.*

But as I touched his skin, there was no waxy film of stage makeup, no slight bump to indicate prosthetics. It felt like the world stood still as I ran my fingers down the sharp slope of his cheekbones, along the square line of his jaw until I got to… His breath was coming in faster now, in little pants, as I pushed my fingers up to touch his tusks.

"Ouch!" I said, snatching my hand back when the sharp point pricked my finger, yet the fleeting investigation had confirmed my suspicions but in no way reassured me. It was hard, had that flat, enamel feel teeth had, but was way sharper. I looked down at the spot of blood on my finger, and somehow, that was what it took to ram home my current situation.

I wasn't in Kansas anymore. I was sitting in the cave home of three orcs, in a realm that had three moons. Fuck.

And while my guard was down, Ghain's hand snapped out, drawing my injured finger up. To the sounds of his comrades' protests, he put my finger in his mouth and sucked away the blood—soft, sensual, slow, sucking. Initially, I just stared, until his eyes fell closed, the lids fluttering slightly.

"Ghain, you go beyond the laws of propriety!" Vargan snapped, surging to his feet and hauling Ghain away from me. "This is first courting!"

"What the fuck is first courting? What the hell is this place? What country am I in?" I asked in a plaintive voice. I think it was the sound of it cracking that had the lot of them turning my way.

"When a woman comes to the orc lands, she is seeking mates," Kren said in a much calmer voice. "The first orc warriors that find her can then try to entice her to stay with them through first courting." His eyes met mine, and the look was startlingly intimate in a way that had my breath seizing in my chest. "If the woman accepts this offer, they have a full turn of the moons to try and persuade her to stay, to make her theirs."

"Theirs..."

I looked down at the horn in my hand, the water now rippling in the container from the shaking of my hand. I took a sip, then a great big mouthful, guzzling the water down until it was empty. Hydrate, yep, gotta stay hydrated. Kren reached out, that same careful gesture, to take the empty horn.

"Is this...?" I stared at the horn, taking in all the brown and black striations on the sides of it, admiring the high polish the craftsman had managed to achieve. "Is this first courting?"

I gestured to the horn, to the water, to the pillows, to the fur, to Ghain, who was now sprawled across the floor, his weight resting on his elbows, looking somewhat chastened. Kren stared at me and then nodded slowly.

"We would offer you aid and protection no matter what you decide," Vargan said, striding forward before sitting back down on the floor in front of me. "It is what our mothers would want. If you do not find us pleasing...?"

Oh Jesus fucking Christ, were we doing this right now? Was the massive, muscle-bound dude who was the devil with that sword-axe thing offering me an out? My mind began to race, putting two and two together, then looking over the three of them with fresh eyes.

One, they really were orcs. My finger had stopped bleeding, but yeah, I had my proof there. Two, taking human women as mates seemed suuuuper important, if they were prepared to make me essentially a marriage offer after just rescuing me, which told me something. Were women rare commodities here? Were there female orcs? I asked them just that.

Vargan frowned, shaking his head, as if the idea was so ridiculous, it was difficult to countenance. That was a no then.

"Orcs are the moons' children, humans, children of the sun. Mating is where we come together. That is the way of things."

"But it doesn't happen very often?"

I asked the question almost fearing the answer, and sure enough, a pensive air fell across the cave. For a moment, there was only the crackle of the fire and the faint whistle of a breeze.

"The humans have never been good at following the law," Vargan said, staring at the fire. "They misunderstand the natural balance. They take the plains, we take the forests and the mountains."

"But now they encroach into our territories, cutting down trees," Kren grumbled.

"Or hacking open the sides of mountains, looking for the stones that shine," Ghain said with a look of disgust. "Their hunger knows no bounds. They have no restraint. And the treatment of the women…"

His eyes went soft and wide in a way that shouldn't have been possible for such a massive manly creature, and yet there he was.

"They come to us, the women, beaten and whipped or broken on the inside. Men do not adhere to the rules of first courting, buying and selling their women like cattle. A father of daughters has a valuable commodity that can fetch a high coin at market."

"In the old days, women were tithed to us," Kren said. "They were brought here in carts and presented to the high chieftain. A feast would be held for seven days and nights, and all bands looking for mates would present themselves to the women. Then they would choose who they wished to be courted by. We keep the human lands safe. We stop the raiders!"

"Peace, brother," Vargan said, putting his hand on the other orc's arm. "This is a weighty conversation, and the hunter moon begins to fall in the sky. We must rest. All decisions and explanations can wait until the morning. Will that satisfy you, Lay-la?"

"Uh, yeah," I replied. He was right—now the adrenalin was gone, I was trashed and sure to wake up with a shocking headache and without the aid of Nurofen either. "So do you guys have a spare bed I could…"

They got to their feet, towering over me, moving apart until I could see the massive bed of sorts at the back of the cave. It was made of carved wood and some sort of vine for slats, with a mattress made of what? Fleece? Dried grass? I didn't know. It was piled high with cured skins and lengths of fabric.

"So that's obviously where you would sleep," I said. "But where would a guest sleep if they had come to stay at your very nice cave?"

"A woman must be protected until she is marked," Vargan said very seriously. "Our mothers would never allow an unmated woman to sleep alone."

"You want me to…"

"She thinks we mean to mate her," Kren said, his eyes flicking between Vargan and me, and dammit, didn't that put a mental picture in my head? They were half fucking naked as it was, only wearing wrist guards and some sort of loincloth, all that very big, very splendid muscle on display, but in bed? I saw myself wedged in between them, their hard bodies pressed… Kren's nostrils flared, and his lips curled somewhat. "And she is not repulsed by the idea."

His voice became all low and raspy and fucking sexy and… No. No, no, no, no! Sleep. I wanted sleep and nothing else.

"We will sleep," Vargan said decisively. "No mating, Lay-la. That is not how first courting goes."

"Awesome, so glad we're on the same page there," I replied brightly, getting to my feet and dusting my hands off on my dress. Fuck, this dress. How the hell was I going to sleep in this bloody thing and the shapewear of doom? But sleeping attire was the least of my problems.

"Not unless you choose us, all of us, Lay-la." Vargan's eyes turned molten brown at that, raking down my bedraggled form. "Then you will get all the mating you can take, and perhaps a bit more."

Well, fuck.

Chapter 6

"Ah, OK..." I stood beside the massive bed, sure I'd need help to clamber into it, and where exactly did I go?

"You lie in the middle," Ghain said helpfully. "As warriors, we will protect you from all sides."

"But you must want to change into a nightgown," Kren said. The other orcs' heads jerked up at that. "My mother always wore one," he explained.

"And where would we procure such a thing?" Vargan asked stiffly. Obviously, he felt like he had been caught out, but Kren walked over to a sturdy-looking chest, pulling it open before producing a nightgown that would've made my nana proud, made of white cotton and cut in a voluminous style. Kren walked over to bring it to me.

"Um...thanks, Kren," I said, taking the garment with more than a little gratitude. I'd had some dickheads slag me off in a club, gone through an interdimensional portal, witnessed a territorial fight between orcs, and yet strangely, the most painful thing was this damn shapewear. It had gone from smoothing and shaping to trying to squeeze my internal organs out like a tube of toothpaste. "Is there somewhere I can get dressed?"

Two of them moved restlessly, as if this was an uncomfortable question, but Ghain was helpful.

"Modesty," he told the others. "Women do not like to show their bodies freely in the beginning."

'In the beginning'?

"Yep, totally modest," I replied. "Just need somewhere private to put this beautiful nightgown on and—"

"This way," Vargan said stiffly, leading me farther into the cave. I marvelled at the rooms that had been created within it, the raw rock carved and shaped to create what looked like a kitchen then a bathroom, and that was where I was led. Only issue was, no door.

"Ah, I need you to…" I made a vague shooing motion.

"I will stand guard," Vargan said, moving into the doorway, the bathroom seeming a whole lot smaller when he did so.

"From what? Giant spiders? Shit, please don't tell me there's giant spiders in here."

"No." That was all he said before turning around and facing the hallway.

Right, so I guessed this was all the privacy I was going to get. I worked fast, restraining a groan when I peeled the dress and then the shapewear off, folding them up and putting them on a spare ledge. As much as I wanted to yeet them into the sun, they were all the clothes I had right now, but as I pulled the nightgown over my head, I noticed two things.

Someone had spent considerable time making it. It had a fineness and lightness to the fabric, the stitches tight and barely able to be seen by the naked eye, except for the beautiful embroidery that had been sewn around the neckline. The other thing was while this was airy and comfortable in ways my dress was never going to be, it was also quite transparent. The low light in the room came from a lantern hung up on the wall, but sure enough, the lines of my body could be seen through the fabric. I crossed my arms firmly across my chest and then cleared my throat to let Vargan know I was done. He turned around, and for a moment, I had a hard time deciphering his expression.

He went to say something, to gesture for me to proceed him back to the bed, when he froze, his eyes raking over me. For a second, I was back at the club, being eyed by strangers, weighed up and found wanting, but that was my own bullshit getting in the way because there was no sneer on Vargan's face. He stared as if those big dark eyes could cut through the fine fabric and bare me to him, and as he swallowed hard, I got the feeling that he wanted that very much.

So that was the moment when I flushed, ducked my head, and nearly died from that appreciative male attention, and dear reader, at least some of that happened. I wasn't used to it and it made me feel hopelessly awkward, but while I had no idea why I was in some alternate realm and how I would get back home, there was something freeing about being on another plane. In a whole different world, I could be a whole different person. I didn't have to shy away from Vargan's gaze or even acknowledge that, so I stood tall and stalked out of the bathroom like I was queen of the world or something.

I heard his amused snort but kept on walking until we got to the bed, where whatever courage I'd had deserted me. Ghain was already lying under the covers, patting a space beside him. I glanced around, at the fire, at the chairs they had set up here, even at a big table as a potential bed, but there was nothing for it. It was either sleep on the hard stone floor or in the bed. A wave of crushing tiredness washed over me, pushing discomfort aside and insisting I get some z's. I climbed into the bed, moving over so there'd be enough space for the other orcs, which provoked a small sound of satisfaction from Ghain. He pulled the covers up and over me, enveloping me in a comforting warmth, but then there was this smell.

You'll be thinking poorly tanned hides or BO or something, but that wasn't it. Calvin Klein or Dior or someone needed to find the source of it, because dayum. It was deep, musky, woody, coupled with something wild. I would've thought some sort of herb, maybe? I found myself burying my head into the pillow to seek more of it, but the source became apparent as the other men got into the bed, the lanterns turned down until the only light came from the embers of the fire. They were close, so close, yet making sure to preserve the space around me, even as I got big lungfuls of their scent. These massive, burly orcs? They smelled like masculine heaven, like Old Spice made Chuck Norris the head of their fragrance department. I let out a ragged little sigh, then another, willing myself to sleep, until finally, my body relented.

THEY MIGHT HAVE BEEN careful about my personal space when we went to sleep, but during? That was a whole other matter. I woke up warm, so warm, I was verging on hot. I grumbled a little, my unconscious mind not remembering where I was and who I was sleeping with, so in my half-awake state, I wriggled and sought to push what I thought were too many blankets on my bed, but these blankets fought back. A heavy weight flopped across my waist, hauling me in close, another pressed into my back, making me very aware that these weren't blankets, not unless bed linen got morning wood in this world.

My eyes flicked open, then screwed shut again as the light stabbed into them, but as I cautiously opened them a crack, I was confronted by an expanse of olive green chest—a very hard, very muscular chest. My fingers flexed slightly from where they had been pinned against Vargan, feeling no give whatsoever in his body.

"Mm..." A low grunt was followed by a rasping sensation on my head. Fuck, was he nuzzling me? A heavy leg shifted, wrapping itself around mine and keeping me perfectly immobilised as he...

I dunno if you were wondering if the freaking massive orc dudes were proportional all over? I am happy—or unhappy—to report that they absolutely were. It took me a while to realise what it was, because it felt like he was trying to thrust a baseball bat my way. I'd been about to reach down and push it back when I realised... Then another was pressed into me, against my butt. Holy shit, I was caught between a rock and hard place. I coughed nervously, not entirely sure what to do, especially when starting to wriggle free. Actual groans, long and needy, emerged from the orcs until Kren looked up in irritation, then took in my distressed expression with a smirk.

"Boneheads!" He rapped his knuckles against Vargan and Ghain's skulls, making the two orcs recoil and wake up abruptly. "You are not showing our guest the proper respect. If you can't keep from molesting her in her sleep, we'll have to place bolsters in the bed."

"Not bolsters," Vargan snapped, but he quickly turned to me. "I must beg your pardon, my instincts got the better of me in the night."

"You were so soft..." Ghain said with a sigh.

"You'll all be soft if you don't rise and shine," Kren said, getting out of bed, and whoaaa... Those little leather loincloths did nothing to disguise his own breakfast boner. I jerked my eyes away as he stretched, every muscle on display.

"We have breakfast to prepare," Vargan agreed, pulling away. Why did I suddenly miss that warmth and that scent? I might or might not have surreptitiously pressed my nose into the blankets to recapture some of it.

"Fruit and bread," Ghain suggested. "That's what my mother always liked in the morning."

"We can see if there's any early berries on the bushes by the river, and we have a bag of wheat still," Kren agreed.

"And I'll bring down a deer for dinner. We'll slow roast it all day," Vargan added.

A loud rumble from Ghain had his hand slapping down over his stomach.

"We'll need to take some travel rations to keep the gullet here from alerting our prey of our advance," Kren said.

"Or perhaps I should stay here," Ghain replied. "We cannot leave the cave untended as we would normally."

Vargan and Kren looked at each other, some kind of understanding passing between them.

"You should, this time," Vargan agreed, and it was now I was beginning to wonder if there was a kind of hierarchy within the group. They called themselves a band, but that obviously wasn't the rock kind. "Keep your wits about you and your weapon close by, and sound the horn if you sense anything. If Urzog thought to breach our territory, so might others." His eyes slid to me. "There are too few women coming to the orc lands, and that makes people desperate."

"Of course," Ghain said with a nod.

And so I watched the two men strap on their weapons, the big axe-sword things supplemented with bows and arrows and a disturbing range of knives. They nodded to us and then walked out of the narrow entrance, out into...

"Where are we?" I asked belatedly. "You never told me."

"Lunor," Ghain replied, stoking up the embers and adding firewood to the fire. "You are in the country of Lunor."

He watched me struggle free of the bedding, belatedly pulling a fur off and wrapping it around me when I felt the whistle of the wind. It was bloody cold here, yet the orc sat there, bare chested and wearing only enough to preserve his modesty. He got to his feet and picked up one of the massive carved wooden chairs and set it by the firepit, a carved hollow in the stone floor. I sat down gingerly, instantly swallowed by the huge seat, feeling like a small child as my feet dangled free of the floor.

"You must have questions, many, if you do not know where you are. Where are you from, Lay-la?"

I watched him move around, creating a little pyramid of kindling, then adding bigger and bigger pieces of wood around it.

"A place with one moon," I replied, not sure how else to explain it. Either the orcs lived in rustic splendour off the grid, or this was a low-tech world. He frowned at my answer.

"A place that only experiences a little of the Mothers' grace?" He shook his head. "However you came to be here, this must be the right path for you."

"I was drunk," I said. "I was stumbling through a park and I heard drums and then I fell. I fell…here. I landed at your feet and then… Why the hell would I have landed right there, right in front of you?"

"We scented you on the wind when out hunting," Ghain replied, stepping closer. His eyes had taken on an intense cast, staring deep into mine. "It pulled us away from taking down a painted cat of the size we'd never seen before, but we couldn't resist. We walked, then ran, following that scent…"

"I smell?" I asked, surreptitiously sticking my nose down the front of the dress.

"Oh yes, most beautifully. Of sun warmed grass and flowers in the field and…happiness."

"Happiness?" I thought of the way I was feeling before I came through and decided that the orc must be delusional. Had they ever scented a woman before, if we were so rare? Had they…?

I raked my eyes over Ghain's body. He was so freaking big. If he could've ditched the green skin and the tusks, but mainly the tusks, he would've been able to make a fine living as a thirst trap or an influencer on social media. He could have ruffled that silky black hair, flexing his biceps as he was doing right now, and the money would have rained down. But he had the tusks and the skin, and I wondered how women in this world responded to them.

"So, first courting," I said, operating on a hunch but willing to see where this went. "Is that something an orc does with a woman after he's played the field a bit?"

"Played the field? Do you mean farming? We do cultivate some land, but tend to trade for crops rather than create fields in the forest."

"No, I mean…" *You're gonna do this?* I thought furiously. *You're going to ask about his dating history?* "After you've sown a few wild oats."

"Wild oats?" His nose wrinkled slightly. "We do not have such plants growing here, but the humans grow something of the like on the plains. They make this thick paste from it." His mouth turned down. "I did not find it palatable at all, but we could ask our trading partners for some if you wish it."

"No, sorry, in my world it's a euphemism for…" *Just say it. Get it out on the table or drop this conversation altogether!* "For courting a woman in a nonserious capacity. Just for fun." I let out a little huff of breath at that.

"Courting but not courting? You would not become mates in the end?"

"Usually, neither person expects it to become a permanent thing," I replied. "You're often too young to be considering something that long term. It's kind of like practising for when you find your mate."

"Too young? How young is too young to begin finding your mate in your world, Lay-la?"

"Oh, I guess teens, early twenties, maybe. It depends on the person."

"And how old are you, Lay-la?"

"Twenty-eight," I replied without thinking. A smug smile spread across Ghain's face. He got to his feet, picking up another horn, and filled it with water.

"For you, Lay-la of the One Moon."

He went down on one knee and offered me the drink.

"This is part of first courting, isn't it?" I asked, my throat going really dry.

"Everything is," he replied with an engaging smile. "Until you say yes or no."

Chapter 7

Taking the horn seemed to make Ghain happy. Drinking from it made him even more so, but then he busied himself sweeping out the cave floor, gathering ceramic dishes in preparation for the meal, and waving me away when I volunteered to help. In some ways, I was glad, my head throbbing after last night's excesses, although it was nothing a couple of painkillers, a litre of water, and a cheeky bacon and Egg Mcmuffin from Macca's wouldn't solve.

Unfortunately, we were a long, long way away from the nearest drive-through, which left me somewhat at a loose end. I ended up selecting a long thin piece of charcoal from the dead coals, the fire having been reduced down. I twirled it in my fingers, then pulled one of the flat stones around the fire pit away from the fire to a comfortable distance as I settled down in a crouch beside it, then watched Ghain.

He was aware of my attention. I'd drawn enough models in art school to know that self-consciousness when it came, but while he stiffened, he forced himself to keep sweeping, using a broom constructed of dried grasses and a sturdy carved handle.

As I picked up the charcoal, I felt that feeling that always came over me when I created something.

It was like everything I was just stopped and there were only my eyes as I traced the long lines of the orc's muscular body and the brisk movements of the broom. I had to draw gesturally. He wasn't sitting still long enough for anything detailed, and anyway, the charcoal and the rock were hardly awesome tools, but I caught it, the broad line of his shoulders, the massive span of muscles across his back, the twist of his hips, the shy look he shot this way…

My fingers stilled at that, and I jerked my eyes down at the stone. Huh, not bad. I reached for another rock that was white and gave off a powdery ochre, rubbing my fingertips in it and starting to add the highlights to the drawing. Then I was searching for others to convey the midtones, then—

"Well, well, will you look at that?"

I felt like I had been grabbed by the scruff of my neck, jerking free of my reverie to find the cave was full of people. Vargan carried a dead deer across his shoulders, Kren had a brace of fish and a basket of berries, and then there was her. An older human woman, with a face gone soft and wrinkled, her white hair pulled back under a coloured kerchief. She wore a white shirt with a brown overdress, and she peered down at my drawing.

"That's the very like of Ghain. You must be a fine lady, to be able to draw so well. What're you doing out in the orc lands?"

"Mother, perhaps you should introduce yourself first," Vargan said with a sigh.

"Perhaps I should," she replied with a smile. "It's been a long time since I've met a newcomer from the lowlands. I'm Judith, mother of Vargan."

"I'm Laila."

When she offered her hand, I held mine up, covered with soot and ochre as they were, but she took it anyway, smiling.

"You are considering my son's offer of first courting?"

Oh, so it was straight to the point time, was it?

"I'm still trying to work out what that is and where I am, to be blunt," I said, getting to my feet. I held my hands out to my sides, not wanting to mark the white cotton gown.

"Well, you can't do that in your nightgown, much as these boys might enjoy that," she said briskly, then turned to the orcs. "Kren, you know you gave her your mother's mating nightgown. It's near transparent for that reason."

The orcs were conspicuously quiet at that, which was ironic, as she barely came up to their belly buttons. She planted her hands on her hips, then bustled over to the chests lined up against the far wall. She flipped through them, coming out with clothing that looked much like her own before nodding.

"Come along then, Lay-la." she said, sweeping me along and back into the bathroom. Once inside, she moved around and retrieved a plug and what looked like a glass jar of bath salts. She turned a big copper spigot that allowed water to flood into a tub that had been carved from raw stone. "These are elf charmed," she said of the bath salts. "Be sparing with them, as they will heat the water considerably." I just blinked as she sprinkled a few in, steam instantly beginning to rise from the water. "Well, off with the gown then."

"Ah, now?" I asked.

"Well, there's no time like the present, is there? Do you not wash each other's hair where you are from?"

"Not since I was a little girl," I replied, eyeing the warm depths longingly. A hot bath would help take the edge of the pain in my head, I was sure.

"Past time, then," she said. "In you pop, and you can tell me more about this place you are from."

Well, OK then.

The idea filled me with fear, I didn't mind saying. I hated taking off my clothes in front of anyone. Doctors, nurses, lovers, friends... Honestly, it didn't matter who it was, I didn't want to do it, but I had filthy hands, was hungover, and Judith seemed pretty determined, so off with the gown it was. I plucked at the fabric carefully, so Judith just shook her head with a smile and then whipped it up over my head.

"Get in," she said with all the weary amusement of a mother, and when I did, sinking into perfectly warm water tight up to my chin, she slapped a bar of soap down in my hand and then pushed my head back to wet it.

"Oh!" Soap of a different kind was worked into my hair once I was sat up again, and whilst I was initially kinda uncomfortable, it didn't take long for me to try and persuade myself that this was just like going to the hairdressers. She worked her hands through my hair with strong confident fingers, a little groan escaping me at the scalp massage I was getting.

"See," she said in a chiding tone. "Now, tell me what to expect with your kin. Do they know you came to the orc lands? Were you running here to escape a man too handy with his hands? Are you highborn? That poses a whole other set of problems, but we have our ways. Girls are usually reticent to talk when they get here, but the more honest you are, the better we can protect you."

"I'm…I'm not from here."

"Well, of course you're not, dearie. No woman is. We're from the plains—"

"No, I mean I'm not from the plains."

"Not from the plains…" Her hands stopped for a second, then began to move much more slowly. "Then where are you from? You're not a raider girl, are you?"

"I don't even know what a raider is," I replied, sitting up straight now. I scrubbed my hands, sending charcoal stained suds into the bath. "I didn't know what an orc was before now, and where I'm from, we use water heaters, not elf crystals to have a hot bath." I looked back over my shoulder, and Judith was very still, eyes wide. "I'm not from this country and not of this world."

Her hands slapped down on the stone rim of the bath.

"You're one of those visitors. We've got another one here.

Soo-zee, Mate of Mahk. Used to talk of weird, impossible things she'd seen at home."

I spun around in the water, sending it lapping at the edge of the bath.

"There's someone else here from my world?"

She nodded slowly.

"We used to make fun of her stories when we were girls, thinking it was some strange conceit of hers."

"I need to talk to her. I need to get back home!"

Suddenly, I thought of Mum and Dad and my brother, John. I thought of my boss and my workmates, and fuck, Hannah! I'd just walked out on her! She'd have to be frantic. I washed off my hands, then scrubbed at my face, the headache just getting sharper and more intense. I'd gone to all the trouble of going out with Hannah, only to what? Storm off like a child? She'd given me an out, let me know she'd take an Uber home with me, and I'd… I let out a long, ragged sigh. I felt like our friendship was slipping through my fingers, but any attempt to hold it tighter seemed to just make things worse.

"I have family and friends who have to be worried for me," I said. "How do I talk to Mahk's mate?"

"It's not as easy as it is on the plains. I used to wander up the road to my friends' houses all the time, going a-visiting. The orcs, they are a territorial lot. Permission must be sought."

"So how do I seek it?" I asked, my voice beginning to rise.

"I'll send word to Mahk. He'll grant you access to Soo-zee and his lands, but he won't be pleased. It took her a long time to settle." Judith's mouth became a thin line, her eyes filling with pain. "Mahk's band ended up abandoning the two of them due to how long it took her to accept their suit. She cried and cried…" Judith wiped her hands on a cloth folded up by the bath. "He may not let you come."

"OK."

My voice was little more than a whisper as I sank down into the bath.

"Turn around." Judith's voice was much gentler. "No point in leaving a job half done."

Together, we washed me clean, but when I emerged from the bath, I felt considerably more subdued. I put on my bra and the underwear Judith supplied me with and then the shirt and overdress, instantly feeling a lot warmer.

"There, pretty as a button," she said, looking me up and down. "Come on then. Those idiots will be falling all over themselves to provide you with a breakfast fit for a queen."

She was mocking the boys in the way of all female relatives who've seen you grow up, but there was an edge of sadness to it. Whatever she knew of Soo-zee… Shit, her name had to be Susie. Whatever Susie had gone through, it didn't make her optimistic about me being here. Because unlike the women who ran or decided to come to the orc lands to find a mate, she was dumped here and had obviously never found a way to go home. That knowledge? It made my steps heavier, my feet dragging as I emerged out into the open living area of the cave.

The orcs looked up, having set up a hot plate across the fire, and were cracking eggs and cooking strips of steak on it, as well as little flattened cakes of unleavened bread. Judith was right—they were ridiculously proud, working together to spoil me. So I plastered on a grateful smile, because I was. God only knows what would have happened to me if I'd come across Urzog and his band, not these three.

Problem is, grateful is not happy.

Chapter 8

Breakfast, unfortunately, was a subdued affair. For great hunking lunks of guys, they were remarkably sensitive, picking up my mood and Judith's as food was handed out. I was served first, then Judith, before they would serve themselves, but I noted more meat and eggs were placed on the grill. Big hunks had to need a lot of fuel. So in the end, I got my bacon and egg McMuffin, just the orc version. The meat wasn't bacon, but it was still flavourful, having been marinated in a combination of herbs I didn't recognise but still liked.

"More, Lay-la?" Kren asked, moving forward to take my plate when I was done.

"No, I'm fine," I said, getting up to take my plate down to the kitchen to wash, but Kren's frown stopped me where I was. Judith just cackled.

"They say the way to a man's heart is through his stomach," she said. "Orcs are the proof of that. Everything is about food. They hunt and forage for the best foods, maintain good stocks of food on their lands. Every celebration centres around food, every important event is marked with a feast, but it's also the language of love. They'll stuff you fuller than a turkey in winter if you let them."

She patted her own bulging belly, not seeming worried by her soft shape in the least.

"It's OK, Kren. I'm not hungry."

"It's a sexual thing too," she added, the words coming out of an old lady's mouth making me go very still, turning stiffly to face her, anything to avoid Kren's intent eyes. Those dark depths seemed to tell me a very explicit story that I was not at all ready for.

"Really?"

I couldn't seem to stop myself from asking, digging myself deeper in the hole.

"Provide, protect, procreate—that's what motivates a man, a good man, anyway," she said. "And orckind? They learn the ways of the war from their fathers but the ways of women from us. We raise our boys to be good men. I'll say this, if you decide to stay. Many a girl is brought up to fear the orc now, their fathers seeking to keep them close, but you'll find none truer. The focus of the whole band will be on you. The strength of their arm, the sweat of their brows all for the purpose of keeping you and any children you bring into this world safe. Better than some human bastard with hard hands, a limp prick, and a preference for pissing away the family's coffers at the alehouse, like my father."

She shook her head stiffly.

"Come then, if you've finished, and leave the dishes to the loyal Kren. My sons asked me to come and instruct you in our ways, as we always do when a new woman comes into the orc lands. I'll tell you about the nature of first courting and then leave you to make up your own mind."

"Mother…" Vargan said in a low growl.

"And you can follow with your bloody great axe if that will give you peace of mind, but at some distance, mind. I'll not have you looming over a girl, making her decisions for her," Judith snapped.

"As you say, Mother."

"You'll need to send a bird to Mahk as well though." Her expression changed, became sadder, more resigned as she stared into her son's eyes. "Lay-la is an outsider, just as Soo-zee is."

Silence fell over the room, but Vargan nodded, getting to his feet and moving to put his plate in the adjoining kitchen, before lifting up his axe. It didn't look like an axe to me, but that was what they'd called it. He gestured for us to lead the way, and Judith tucked my arm in hers, taking me outside to show me a whole other world.

IT HAD BEEN TOO dark for me to see much of this place the night before, only the three moons, but as we stepped outside, I was struck by how beautiful it was. A path had been cut into the mountainside, leading from the cave down to the forest below. Above us, long pipes led from the top of what looked like a mountain.

"It's where they get their water from," Judith explained, taking me down the steps. "And why it's so blasted cold. I endured ice baths for years before it was explained what the elf salts do, which is why I'm talking to you now. Do you know why it's called first courting?"

"Ah, no."

"The first orcs who find a woman can put themselves forward as her beaus, court her and try to persuade her to take them as her mates. They are the first to do so—"

"So that's why it's the first courting," I said. "So if she's not keen?" I thought of Urzog and shuddered. "Other orcs step forward?"

"A woman seeking orc mates will always find one. She can go through second courting, third, fourth. However long it takes, there will be bands that step forward. What is frowned upon is rejecting a band and then coming back to them to try courting again." Judith took a sidelong look at me. "You don't seem like one of those flibbertigibbet girls who likes to play with a man, but you should know that that kind of behaviour will not be received well here."

She looked over her shoulder to where Vargan trailed at a respectful distance.

"They are creatures of strong passions, have hearts that will carry them into impossible battles with little care, but they can be hurt." Her gaze returned to me, even and warm brown. "They can be hurt right to the quick. There's no point pretending to entertain things with them if your heart is not ready."

We stopped just before the tree line, a forest spanning out before us.

"I can't," I said. "I have a family to get back to, a life. I didn't enter the orc lands running from an abusive husband or an arranged marriage. I was drunk, unhappy, and I staggered into a park and found myself here."

"They'll find that hard to accept," Judith said with a sigh, then drew me deeper into the forest.

A strange calm settled over me as we walked along a meandering path, the rustle of the breeze in the leaves and the sounds of birds singing somehow lightening the mood. It wasn't hard to convince myself that I was back home, in my world, wandering through bushland.

"They believe no woman comes to the lands without reason. Their belief system about the Mothers? It's all centred on this. They say that the world was one of darkness and light, the sun during the day and then at night, nothing. Absolute darkness fell, and in that, the dark things crept out. The orcs were the only defenders of the land, battling the beasts that came from the bowels of the earth that prey on the sleeping under cover of darkness. Then they came."

She stopped for a second, reaching out and capturing a seed that fell from a tree, the strange little thing sporting this kind of twin blade on the top that let it spiral through the air, lazily riding the breeze to find its final destination.

"Three women, from where, they do not know, but they

came into the lands, and with them came moons' light. Darkness was driven back and so were the creatures, and in their gratitude, the orcs fell to their knees before these three beautiful women, pledging their allegiance."

She flung the seed back out into the air, and we watched it spiral off.

"Bands of orcs, brothers, or brothers-in-arms, came forward and begged the women to stay, offering them food, shelter, and the strength of their arms. Whatever they wanted."

"The origin of first courting," I said.

"Just so. There are no women born to orcs, which of course makes you wonder where they came from in the first place? Did they spring from the mountains themselves? That would make sense, what with their rock-hard heads." She chuckled as she cast a look over her shoulder to where Vargan stood up the track, scanning the forest for threats. "But their hearts are as constant as the mountains too. An orc lives, loves, fights, with all he has."

"So what was the deal with Urzog?" I asked, remembering the mountain man of last night.

"Pfft, him. Waste of air, that old bastard. He and his band of idiots are outcasts, living on the fringe of the lands, harassed by the humans, rejected by the orcs. His name is not spoken amongst polite society."

Judith looked up at me.

"Every society has rules and values they hold dear, but there's always those that come out...wrong. My da was one of them. My mother was a beautiful girl, much too good for the likes of him, and he beat her daily for that crime, trying to bring her down to his level. Urzog is the same. Being such a big bastard, so strong, he thought that meant something, that he was due more respect, more women, more lands. Imagine his disappointment when he got none of those things." She nodded. "If he's sniffing around, then I understand my son's wariness. He does not adhere to our laws. But..."

She patted my arm, and then we started walking down the path again.

"You will be safe with my son and his band. He has fought for your honour already?"

"Ah, yeah."

"And he will again. Stay on their land, and you will be safe. Now, if you have a need for me." We turned down a side path, and as we walked, I saw a log cabin emerge, with a very nice veranda, a rocking chair set up on the front. "I cannot live within their cave and my band died fighting the raiders, so my son, my sons really, though I only birthed the one of them, they built me this place. They keep me safe, bring me food, come and sit on my porch and listen to my stories, and stop an old woman from going mad from the memories of lost love. They urged me to consider another band, to go through first courting again, but I couldn't."

She let me go now, moving to stand in front of me and smiling.

"You'll have a lot of questions, being an outlander. Ask one of my boys to bring you my way if you do. Even if it's just how to stop their interminable snoring." She cackled at that. "Or to learn my famous carrot cake recipe."

She winked at me, making me laugh, but her expression became serious again.

"Let them know your decision about first courting. I don't know what it must be like, to come from a whole other world to this…" She shook her head. "But tell them. Soo-zee did not, not until it was too late, and it ate her up inside. They are very taken with you, but they will accept your decision."

I was going to say something, so many things. The first was a knee-jerk reaction to deny any attraction between the orcs and me, but that was just dumb. I'd been woken up by very obvious evidence. The second was to reiterate my need to get back home, but she knew that, and soon, the orcs would know too. The third was just sadness. This place was fucking wild and so beautiful. My fingers itched for paints and chalk and paper, so much paper. I needed to record all of it, which reminded me… My phone, it had to be back in the cave. The one good thing about the dress was it had pockets. I had specified as such to Hannah. I looked behind me, saw Vargan standing there, axe resting on the ground, his hands on the haft.

"Thank you, Judith," I said. "You're an amazing hair washer."

That was lame, so fucking lame, but she just cackled in response, taking my hand and giving it a squeeze.

"Sometimes, we need to let others do what we can do ourselves. It gives them pleasure to give it and us to receive. You're a good girl, just treat them right, and the Mothers will look after you."

When she turned to go, I walked back to Vargan, rehearsing in my mind what to say. 'It's not you, it's me' probably didn't translate in the same way here, did it? I was so caught up in my head, I jumped when Vargan put his hand on my shoulder.

"Lay-la, I was wondering if I might show you something?"

Call me insecure, call me desperate for masculine attention, but when I looked up into those deep brown eyes, all my rehearsed conversations went out the window. I saw it—the gentle offer, the hand outstretched, just waiting, waiting for me to say yes. So I opened my mouth and said just that.

Rejecting the orcs? That was for future Laila to worry about. Right now, I was Lay-la, and she was transfixed by the slow smile that spread across the giant orc's face.

Chapter 9

"Oh my god," I said as we stepped out of the tree line to emerge into an open field of flowers. It was still on the mountainside, the croplands not beginning until much farther down, but right here? It was beautiful. I walked closer in a big rush, then stopped myself, looking back at Vargan.

He smiled down at me with an almost shy look. Well, as shy as a massive freaking orc could be, but he looked terribly, terribly pleased before holding out a hand to me. It was a massive paw, complete with long talons, but I found myself stepping up and taking it anyway, mine no doubt feeling like a child's in his palm. He drew me farther in, the flowers' heady scent rising as we passed, and I couldn't stop exclaiming at the rainbow of colours.

Some were big yellow fluted flowers, others little white daisy-looking ones, yet others were blowsy red ones, a bit like a combination of a poppy and a rose, and just as sweet smelling. I let the orc take me into the depths of the field until he suddenly decided this was the place to sit down. I plopped down into the grass, but Vargan, he laid his axe down beside him and sprawled out in the flowers, crushing some to my dismay. He just plucked a strand of grass, putting it between his lips to chew before lying down flat on his back, letting the sun's rays caress him.

"My mother spoke to you of first courting," he said, right when I thought he'd dropped off to sleep or something. It was warm and the air was hazy, and I admit, I felt a little drowsy too.

"She did."

"And what say you, Lay-la, daughter of Tray-cee?"

This was ten out of ten not the place I thought I'd be in right now. My throat began to work, the expectation that I answer him there, pushing at me, but what did I say? Judith had told me about Susie for a reason, to prevent her own son from experiencing the same pain as Mahk, and I owed it to him, to all of the band, to save them from that.

"I'm not of this world," I said.

"No, you are like the Mothers." His eyes opened a crack and were so warm and lazy right now, I just wanted to dive into the dark depths. "You bring light to the darkness."

"But unlike the Mothers, I need to get back somehow," I replied. "I have a family that love me, that will be worried sick about me, and if I stay here…"

He just stared for a moment, his gaze soft and unjudging. I watched his eyes take in everything I was, studying me like I was a book with all the world's knowledge in it, and waited…for what? For judgement, for anger, for an expectation that I give him something I knew I couldn't, because most of the time, that was how it seemed everyone treated me, but it never arrived. He gave me a little quirk of a smile, made a whole lot scarier with those tusks, and then asked me the question that floored me.

"If you could see your family and your friends freely, like the women of Lunor do, would you consider first courting?"

For a moment, I just stared at him, taking in all the ways he was completely alien to me and all the ways he wasn't. His thick brow, his heavy bone structure, the sharp slope of his cheekbones. The swirling tattoos carved into his dark green skin. His talons, his tusks, sure, but there was also his thick black hair, bound back into braids, tiny silver clasps bound around many of them, a lot of them engraved with some glyphs. As my eyes slid down to take in that massive chest, I was pretty sure he flexed his muscles to make sure he looked as impressive as possible, and a little laugh escaped me, because he did.

"Yeah, I think I would."

A hand shot up, grabbing me by the shoulder and pulling me down, down, into the hollow of his collarbone. My hand jerked up, then came to rest on his chest, the strange sensation of touching him resonating all the way through me. His skin felt tougher, thicker, but as I gave it an experimental little stroke, I decided I quite liked it. I liked the way his arm tucked me closer into the side of his body. I liked the heavy weight of it and the way his nails traced little circles on my flesh.

"Then we will find a way for you to see your family and friends whenever you wish," he said, moving in closer until he nuzzled my hair. "So we may begin first courting."

Fuck, if this wasn't first courting, I was in deep, deep shit. As he did that, my body went limp against his, feeling small, soft, and protected. That, and the soft beat of the sun down on my skin, meant I didn't want to move anywhere right now.

"Agreed, Lay-la?"

"Mm-hmm…" I mumbled, breathing his spicy scent in.

Chapter 10

Of course I couldn't just chill with Vargan in the sun, then stumble onto the lost stone of Blah di Blah that instantly opened a portal between my world and his. A permanent one, of course, so I could duck home, see the parental figures, hang with Hannah, and then go back to the Wonder Cave of Orc Gang Bangs afterwards. Nothing could be that easy. Instead, I woke up as Vargan went very, very stiff beneath me.

"Stay still, my Lay-la," he said in a harsh whisper. My eyes flicked open in earnest now as I heard what had disturbed him—a low rumbling growl. He rolled into a crouch, his axe in hand, and for a second, I shamefully admit, I was a little turned on. He was a picture of masculine strength, eyeing the landscape beyond until his focus narrowed. He rose up slightly, the muscles in his thick thighs taut, his axe at the ready. He patted my knee, as if to indicate I needed to stay put, and then he moved.

You know the bloody awful sounds cats make when they are fighting? Like, the yowling and the screaming and the messy jumble it all takes when they are in full-on battle mode? That was what this sounded like, but a million times louder. I peeped above the tops of the flowers and saw Vargan move like lightning, running towards something that looked like a leopard and a tiger had a baby.

Lean like a leopard, but with a ruff like a tiger, its striped ears flattened against its skull as it howled its disdain, but the scary thing was that its focus shifted away from Vargan, which didn't make sense. As he was attacking, its evil green eyes zeroed in, its body coiling and sprinting from a dead start, straight toward me. I caught Vargan's confused expression as the beast ignored him. The orc pivoted in mid-air, landing with a graceful thud before pelting back towards me. I couldn't see what he was doing, and a scream built in my throat, all the adrenalin in my body howling at me to get to my fucking feet, soldier, and move, but I couldn't. Fight, flight, or freeze, and I'd chosen freeze, staring at the bloody cat like I was a stunned fucking mullet.

It yowled its hatred, fangs bared, tongue slavering as its back legs coiled, and then it sprung into the air, coming flying towards me. It would have all gone so well for the cat. Vargan was behind it, on its tail but not close enough. For a second, I saw it, my life rushing past my eyes, dragging up all my successes and failures and random moments like farting in the bath as a kid, and I realised then I wasn't ready for it to end.

Then a green body slammed into the side of the cat, sending it barrelling across the ground. Kren was up and stabbing at the cat's bare throat in the second it took to recover, and the cat fell limp to the ground.

Strong arms scooped me up, but I could barely feel them. I couldn't feel my face, my skin, my hair, or my hands. All I could do was stare at the scowling Kren, the blood dripping from his blade right up until he flicked it away, and then look down at the glassy eyes of the cat gazing up at the sky.

"You are safe, my Lay-la," a masculine voice said, and with it came a growing realisation. I was tucked up against another masculine chest, a soothing tone saying that sentence over and over. A hand went to my hair, stroking it, as I started to shiver. If I were more kick ass, I would've fought my way free and gone to survey the damage, maybe fist bumped Kren for his good work, but I'm sorry to say, I really wasn't.

If I had to kill my own food, I'd be a vegan for life. I found it hard to kill spiders, for fuck's sake. So I did the very un-kick ass thing of burying my face in the neck of whoever was holding me. *Ghain*, my brain supplied, apparently having a sixth sense about these things, as I just sucked in lungfuls of his woody scent, over and over, until I heard the shouts.

"What in the name of the Mothers were you doing?" Kren shouted. "That was a painted cat! It would've ripped Lay-la to pieces and left her to bleed!"

"They do not come to the grasslands," Vargan replied stubbornly.

"Then what is this? Mother Joan's fat mouser come to play? How could you do this?"

I peeled my face away from Ghain, his eyes drawn down by my movement. He seemed to see something there, letting me down now I was beginning to recover. I straightened my hair, then my dress, and marched over to the two men.

"You are unharmed?" Kren wrenched me closer, searching my face, my body, my hands, for signs of injury. "It did not hurt you?"

"No, and thank you, Kren." He stilled when I placed a hand on his arm, blinking as he just stared at it. I rubbed my hand up and down his muscular forearm, trying to avoid the flecks of blood, but it didn't seem to soothe him. Instead, he just moved closer, crowding into me, blocking my view of the other orcs as they went to deal with the corpse of the cat.

"My heart won't stop racing," he said, placing my hand on his chest so I could feel it, and sure enough, it was. He stared at me intently, like he would memorise every inch of me. "That cat… It leapt…"

"And how did you come to be in the grasslands?" Vargan asked, a little huffy. When Kren turned, I saw Ghain and Vargan were up to their elbows in blood. I couldn't feel sorry for the cat. It had definitely been a case of it or me, and right now, it looked like it would be made into a very pretty fur blanket as they worked together to skin the animal.

"Lucky we were passing," Kren shot back, but the passing bit didn't sound entirely honest. "You were gone for some time, and we all know Judith would not monopolise Lay-la's time for so long."

Monopolise? Ohh.

Kren turned back to me, not having let go of my hand.

"Let us return to the cave, Lay-la. You must be thirsty and wish for your midday meal."

Well, not exactly, but I wasn't cool with sitting in the pretty grasslands anymore. I nodded to Kren, who smiled and then used my hand to lead me back into the cave.

WHEN WE ARRIVED, I found the cool of the cave refreshing after all that sun. Kren forced me to sit down, then brought me a horn of water to drink. I was sipping that as he busied himself, preparing meat from the deer on the spit I wasn't sure I could eat. Adrenalin had my guts in its grip, squeezing them tight as what happened and what might have been played over and over in my mind. I started to lose my awareness of the cave, the smells of the cooking fire, the sounds of the other orcs as they entered the cave, everything starting to just fade away. Not disappear precisely, just soften, until everything sounded far off and distorted.

Perhaps that was why Kren appeared at my knee. He set the plate of food down on the floor, then stared up at me in concern, removing the still half full horn of water and then collecting me up in his arms. I wanted to protest that I wasn't a doll. I wasn't a child or anything else small and fragile, and yet, here I was. Those protests didn't last long when he swept me up and out of the chair and then onto his lap as he took my place. He held me close and stroked my back and hair, until finally, it all came back again. My brain was ready to deal with reality.

But as Laila came back online, I quickly realised something.

His body was hard all over, and as I shifted, I realised he was more so in one particular place. My eyes darted up in question, and he looked away abruptly, as if embarrassed by his reaction. I guessed getting a hard-on for a girl who wasn't prepared to be courted would be kind of horrifying for him. I didn't like that response, the hurt in his eyes, because I knew all too well what that felt like.

Crushing on people I knew weren't crushing on me, or worse, when I didn't know. When I'd mistaken friendliness for something else and then had my world come crashing down when I realised how wrong I was. So I did something terribly unwise, reaching up and placing a kiss on the corded muscle of his neck, his body freezing as soon as he felt it. When his hands tightened around me, when his head dipped down so he could peer into my eyes, I slipped off his lap.

I couldn't play fast and loose with him, with any of them. I was going to find a way home, and then they would be free to find a nice girl from a nearby village, settle down with someone who could give her whole self to them. I walked down the hallway, ready to go into the bathroom and splash cold water on my face, when I was forced to a stop in the doorway. In the bath were Ghain and Vargan, stripped naked and standing in the water, using it as a pool to wash all the blood and soap off them.

Look away, look away, look away! my brain shrieked, but I didn't, did I? Despite all my complaints and protestations and trying to do the right thing, part of me fucking wanted this, wanted them. My eyes ran across their big, strong forms, caught every shift of their muscles as they moved, saw the way their eyes heated as they caught me watching, slow smiles spreading across their faces. Because, like they say, action talks and bullshit walks. My 'I need to get home' crap was walking on out of the cave, and right now, I was down to build human and orc relations. Their hands started to move much more slowly now, in recognition of their audience, as they rubbed the soap into the skin of their abs, then lower and lower.

So spank me later, but I looked. Of course I fucking looked.

A small, primal, shitty part of myself had to know if these dudes were packing what I thought they were. As I saw the biggest damn schlongs I'd ever seen soft start to twitch, I could confirm that each of these fuckers had girth that would make a Coke can feel inadequate and what looked like an excellent advertisement for Subway footlongs in length.

"Fuck…" I breathed out, ready to apologise, but my throat just seemed to close up, particularly as the orcs started to chub up under all my attention.

"Lay-la…"

Kren called my name and came to stand beside me in the hallway, blocking my way out but not intentionally, not until he saw what was happening. Then he moved ever so slowly closer, so I could feel the heat radiating off his body.

"Lay-la?"

Just the scrape of a nail down the side of my neck, so gently as to make me shiver, was what it took to break the spell. I jerked back from Kren, from the doorway, from all of it, and then ducked under his arm, stumbling out into the living area, waving my hands at my face, trying to cool myself.

"Lay-la."

Kren said my name again, tracking me into the living area at a slow pace, one even I could outrun, until I began to hustle towards the doorway of the cave. Then he moved like lightning, blocking off my path, forcing me to back up or claw at him. I wanted to do the latter, but I did the former, trying so very hard to remember why I was not accepting their very generous offer of providing, protecting, and procreating.

And we were back.

Bringing home the three guys to Mum and Dad. Having them listen to Dad's awkward jokes and the bickering around the dining table at Christmas. Or worse—never having another Christmas again.

"Lay-la," a voice behind me called, and the wet slap of feet on stone let me know everyone was done with their bath.

"You cannot go outside," Kren said. "Not with painted cats around."

"Well I can't stay here," I said, picking at my fingernails. "There's no books to read. No TV. Nothing to draw with."

"If those are what will keep you in the cave, then we will find them," Kren said. "But not now."

He moved in closer, and by the sounds behind me, so did the other two orcs. Sure enough, when I spun around, there they were, wedging me into the space between them.

"I smell your need, Lay-la," Ghain said, his eyes hypnotic in their darkness. "It smells so sweet."

"Sweeter than honey, and I like honey very much," Vargan agreed.

"Awesome, well, if we could maybe all put some clothes on, we can talk about how I smell at length, from opposite ends of the cave," I said. "That way there are no painted cats, I stay in the cave, and no…"

"No what, Lay-la? What don't you want?"

I gritted my teeth, trying very hard to find the words, but I couldn't think, could I? If they could scent me, well, I was getting wafts of them. Feral, male, spicy. My mouth watered with the taste of it, like it was the most delicious thing. Like they were the most delicious things and I just needed—

"You are our guest," Kren said, tipping my chin up towards him. "Your needs are ours to fulfil. This is what we have been taught by our mothers."

"I'm fairly sure your mothers didn't teach you what I'm thinking," I muttered, remembering this morning and the way we were all wedged together, but this time, there were no loincloths or nightgowns in the way. The orcs groaned as they pressed in closer, whatever I was thinking triggering something in them, which was not helping.

"We know how to see to a woman's needs," Vargan insisted. "No mating."

This comment was directed at the others more than me.

"I can't, Vargan," I said, fighting for breath. "I need to go home, to go back to my family."

"But not today." One of those claws ran down my breastbone, moving lower until it met the neckline of the dress. "Nothing can be done today."

It couldn't, could it? Like, where would I even start and what could I do?

"Not today," I agreed, my muzzy head beginning to swim.

"To try and persuade a woman to accept first courting," Ghain said, moving behind me, running his hands down my shoulders. "A band will bring a woman gifts, demonstrate their prowess in tournaments, show them the splendour of their cave, bring them riches from the depths of the mountains, but the most persuasive thing an orc can bring is always his tongue."

"His tongue?" I asked, frowning, but my answer appeared quickly enough. His flicked inside my ear, something I never really got into before, but right now, a long mobile wet force probing a dark place, then retracting? The meaning was clear, and I shuddered in response.

"And that isn't against the rules?"

"It's very much a part of the rules," Kren said. "How else do you think we woo women away from the men? They care not for a woman's pleasure, but us? We like to feast on it."

And *Sold!* to the quivering girl from another world with very sticky thighs.

Chapter 11

One little sound of acquiescence from me, and I was scooped up again and swept over to the side of the bed. Hands moved everywhere, removed my dress, then my shirt, but I stopped them at my bra as self-consciousness flooded in. I glanced up, desperately trying to read their faces and seeing the very affirming heat in their eyes. I consciously took a deep breath and then undid my bra, letting it fall to the ground and my breasts to spill out.

"Ach, Lay-la, are all women of your world so blessed?" Kren ground out, walking closer and tracing a claw down the slope of my breast. Then he cupped both of them, seeming to find it very satisfying that my cups runneth over, even in his huge hands. "You must assure us they aren't, or my people will overrun yours and steal all your women."

Kisses along the back of my neck, hands stealing over my body, made it impossible to answer him.

"Feast, brother," Vargan said as he nibbled his way along my neck and across my shoulders. "Have your taste because we long for ours."

That seemed to be all the incentive Kren needed. He placed glancing kisses along my chest, the cool brush of his tusks reminding me this wasn't just some dude. When my hand went to his shoulder, then his head, to steady myself, he paused. His eyes fluttered closed at that small touch, just for a moment, before he recovered himself and continued.

"This is the body of the Mothers," he said, rubbing the flat of his thumbs across my nipples, making me jerk from the sensation. I felt as jumpy as a cat and twice as horny. Sharp talons closed over both nipples, pricking deep enough to make me shiver, but no more than that. Then talons were replaced by lips, closing around an aching point and sucking it into his mouth.

"Holy shit!" I yelped at the rush of feeling. His suction was strong, pulling in long, slow intervals that made my clit pulse helplessly, my cunt closing down on a distressing nothingness. A small whine escaped me, which had the three of them chuckling.

"We will take our guest to our bed to pleasure her," Vargan ordered, and Kren's mouth popped free as he looked, unfocused, at the rest of us. It was like he was caught in some sensual haze, and I was right there with him. A very naked, very hard Vargan picked me up and laid me across the middle of the bed, the other two following quickly behind. I took all of them in, my eyes jerking from one orc to another, my hands reaching out, though I couldn't work out for which, but they were batted away.

"This is for your pleasure," Ghain explained, bending over and pressing a kiss to my forehead, then my lips when I tilted them up to meet his.

His eyes went wide, and I felt mine do the same. Part of me had wondered how you kissed a guy with prominent lower teeth, but it was apparently easier than I'd thought. It was a careful process, sure. There'd be no slamming lips down on lips with an orc, but as his lips parted, I slipped my tongue in, much to his surprise.

His hand went around my skull, holding me closer as the kiss got deeper and deeper, but the others weren't content to wait. I felt a weight settle on the bed between my legs, another by my side, hands skimming up my thighs, tracing circles around my nipples until I was forced to jerk away.

Talons were cool and shit when playing, but near my vag? I didn't want an involuntary genital piercing any time soon. Vargan chuckled from where he lay between my thighs, then very conspicuously bit down his talons to blunt nails. He waggled them in the air. "Mated men rarely let their talons grow long," he explained with a smug look. "It is a sign of domestic bliss." Then he reassured me by dragging those blunted fingers down my thigh.

There was no pain, no scratchiness, and I went limp against the bed as the damn orcs started chuckling again. The others followed Vargan's lead, divesting themselves of their talons before stroking me everywhere. I was caught up in a sensual delirium, those massive hands caressing me everywhere.

So you might be wondering how I transitioned from insecure Laila in the club to this sex goddess, starfished out on the bed and worshipped by orcs. Maybe you're thinking it was their otherworldliness that made it OK for me, but really, it was something else. Sometimes, I'd stumble onto a sexual partner who was into what I had going on. He'd be obviously appreciative, make subtle but sweet comments about my body and how much he loved it, and while I found it hard to accept entirely, I'd been willing to try. It wasn't that I thought my body was relentlessly hideous. It just was a weird combination of genetics, environment, and factors outside my control, just like everyone else's was. The problem lay in the way society at large perceived it.

Without trying real hard, or even not trying at all, I'd find out exactly what so many people thought. Long stares at me and my shopping trolley when buying food, muttered comments as I passed by on the street, or hollered at me by a scrub in his best friend's ride as they drove past. In the news, in fashion magazines, in the comments on posts on social media. Opinion after opinion stabbed into me, making damn sure I knew where I fit in all of this. So I was able to relax under the hands of these three orcs because rather than throwing me a pity fuck or chatting me up so a friend could get at Hannah, they worshipped me.

Hands cupped and caressed my breasts, teasing the nipples

until the points stood out proud, and then they groaned, dropping their heads down to suckle on them. Lemme tell you, having that done by two men had me dripping. Vargan seemed to sense that, placing kisses along my hip bones and along the crease of my thigh before splitting me open, rubbing his fingers through my folds.

"So wet, my Lay-la. Wet for us."

Like I had any choice in the matter, as he teased my clit. Apparently, the mothers had taught them something, because he found it without issue, stroking the hood until I felt myself starting to drip even more, but he didn't let me make a mess of myself. A broad, thick tongue swept in and up, making my nerve endings sing as he sucked noisily, trying to collect every drop.

"Fuck, brother," Ghain croaked out. "Is she as sweet as she smells?"

"Sweeter," Vargan said with a pant, then used his mouth for much more carnal things.

I felt his tusks press against my pubic mound, anchoring me there as his tongue lashed across my clit, flicking it harder and faster until I started to move restively. My cries of pleasure were swallowed by Ghain, who seemed to think this kissing biz was a damn fine thing, his fingers tightening around my nipple and tugging, while Vargan's lips did the same around my clit. They were all forced to ride the waves of my body as it tensed and relaxed, faster and faster. Then I started to get frantic, feeling empty, so empty.

I needed to thank whomever had put these guys through their paces. A thick finger was pushed inside me, right when I was almost screaming from the need for it, and I was forced to jerk my lips away as it was worked inside me.

"More," Kren ordered. "She needs more."

"She will need a lot more if she is to take us during first mating," Vargan observed, but that barely registered. Another finger was added, giving me a bit of a stretch, but then another was pushed in.

They congratulated each other as my hips lifted off the bed, not realising why. I was so full, I felt overstuffed, and I found myself moaning in response, but was that from discomfort or pleasure? When Vargan curled his fingers up, pressing hard on the spot that just had my fingers clawing at the bed, I made a decision. Pleasure, absolutely pleasure.

"Give us your pleasure, Lay-la," Vargan ordered, his deep voice resonating all the way through me until it felt like my cells themselves sat up and paid attention. It was coming, it was definitely coming, but I couldn't say as much, only able to let out ragged cries over and over again as Kren and Ghain dropped their heads to my breasts again. Coupled with Vargan's wily tongue, I had no choice but to surrender. Then I was coming, bliss rippling through my body in little waves that just got bigger and bigger, the relentless suction of their mouths, the push and pull of Vargan's fingers and the lash of his tongue, all taking the choice from me. My eyes snapped wide, staring blindly at the cave roof as I jerked and twitched, every muscle contributing to the insane riot inside me.

And then, with impossible sweetness, I was stroked and petted down until I was just about a puddle on the bed. I couldn't have been looser limbed, my eyes rolling shut for just a second.

"Did we see to your needs, my Lay-la?" someone asked, and I just nodded, unable to form words, just letting myself sink into the afterglow as they settled around me.

I was wedged tight between the bodies of three orcs, and I couldn't have been happier.

But I wasn't the only one with needs to be seen to. As my heartbeat started to return to normal, I rolled up onto my elbows, staring down at the wondrous carpet of man flesh before me, and saw their cocks were pulled up tight against their bellies, the swollen heads weeping a pearly liquid. I pulled free from their clinging arms, their hands trying to pull me back down again, but I wasn't having that. I rolled Kren, my saviour, onto his back and his eyes went wide.

Somehow, the cocky warrior was gone, and instead, here was

a man on the edge. As I traced my finger down his chest, following the sharp lines of his muscle, Vargan growled.

"No mating, Lay-la. Not unless you accept us as your mates."

"And what does mating entail?" I asked, wrapping my hand around Kren's cock, his head dropping to the bed as he thrust his hips up. "Working your cocks up inside me?"

"Yes…" Kren replied, but was it to my question or my hand?

"So if I don't have penetrative sex, then I adhere to the rules?"

Vargan's expression was mulish, but he nodded.

"We are here to please you, Lay-la, not the other way around," Ghain explained. "It gives us pleasure to do so. You should lie down, let us tend to you, allow us to taste your sweet honey. We will do it again and again until you cannot bear it anymore."

"Tempting," I said, my resolve starting to waver. "And I'm not entirely sure that's off the table."

I turned my focus back to Kren though, my spare hand stroking down the hard cradle of his hips, my fingers dropping down the severe line of the V of muscle there. My other hand gripped Kren's cock tighter, and he groaned instantly in response. There was something about this, a man brought low by something I did, his very frank responses. It made me feel powerful. I watched his stomach muscles flutter as he panted roughly, each in time with my strokes, knowing I did that. And pre-cum? It was apparently much more copious in orcs. It spilled from the top of his cock with every pass of my hand, almost like I was milking it out of him.

"But what if I need this?" I asked, changing my strokes, corkscrewing my palm around his length, making Kren's body go rigid.

"He will come soon if you keep doing that," Vargan observed.

"I think that's the point," I said without turning my head, unable to speak to Vargan directly, the spill of Kren's pre-cum drawing my eye over and over. It was like he was having one long protracted orgasm, again and again. I drew closer, watching the liquid bubble up, only to slide down and slip against my palm. I didn't hate swallowing jizz, but it wasn't one of my top five things I liked doing. Somehow, though, I was drawn closer. That spicy scent of theirs, it got stronger the more I jacked Kren's cock, until finally, my tongue flicked out and I licked the head of his cock clean.

My eyes flicked open as a strange taste, somewhat like pumpkin spice and apples, burst in my mouth. That was freaking weird, but I couldn't clear my head to think too much about it. I went back for more and more, licking Kren's cock clean, then sucking the seed straight from the source.

"Mothers' grace..." Kren ground out. "You feel... That's... Goddesses above, I...!"

"Lay-la, you need to stop," Vargan warned. "If he comes—"

Not if, when. I was sucking him as hard as I could now, bobbing my head, taking him deeper and deeper, which just didn't seem possible, but there it was. However, his dick was taking on that diamond hard feel men got right before they came, his hands coming to rest gently on my skull, his breath panting harder and faster, just as my movements did the same, until he cut through the air of the cave with a godawful roar.

I was about to find out the source of Vargan's concern.

Men ejaculate a couple of teaspoons of jizz, don't let them tell you otherwise. It might get ejected at high velocity and spray everywhere, but there isn't that much of it, trust me. The same could not be said of orckind. My mouth was blasted with rope after rope of Kren's cum, forcing me to frantically swallow or drown.

I could have easily pulled my mouth off, let him make a mess of his stomach, but I didn't want to. Something in me craved this, craved him, so I didn't stop swallowing until Kren lifted me clear. He just stared with eyes of molten chocolate, then rubbed his thumb over my swollen lips, scooping up what had spilled free. When I sucked it clean, he grabbed me, rolling away from the others and curling his body against mine.

"That was..." he said, unable to pull his eyes from me, stroking my hair and face. "Lay-la, I have never felt such pleasure."

"Never?" I said in good humour, thinking this was just pleasing hyperbole, but he didn't smile, didn't chuckle. He just touched me and stared. "Never ever?"

"My band has not been lucky enough to ever go through first courting with a woman. Our territory is not close to the human realm. The women did not choose us at great feasts."

"Never ever..." I whispered the words now, only just getting their meaning. "You're virgins?"

"Ver-gins?" Kren said.

"She means untouched," Ghain said, peering over Kren's shoulder. "Of course we are untouched. An orc saves himself for his mate."

"And until we can find a way to allow Lay-la to revisit her family, she cannot consider becoming our mate," Vargan said. "This is why we were not supposed to indulge. We meet our guest's needs due to the laws of hospitality, but we cannot afford to allow more."

Kren rolled over and took me with him. I let out a little yelp when he wedged me between him and Vargan.

"I dare you to knock Lay-la's hand away when it collars your prick," Kren said, nibbling my ear as my hand reached out to do just that. Vargan stiffened at the contact, but his cock flexed through my fingers quickly enough, and when I squeezed it, his brow knotted, all his former good intentions going right out the window. Maybe this was wrong, maybe I shouldn't be muddying the waters, but right now, I felt strong and powerful because I could reduce a huge warrior down to a drooling mess with just one small caress. "Tell her to stop," Kren pushed. "Tell Lay-la not to touch you."

I got the game the orc was playing, loosening my fingers and making out like I was pulling away, but Vargan's hand slapped down over it, holding me still.

"No, please, Lay-la..."

Yeah, I liked that, I liked breathless begging a whole lot. Ghain watched, wide-eyed, which gave me an idea. I pulled free of Kren, pushing Vargan down on his back, and as I clambered over him, I began to wonder if I'd made the right decision. Vargan's hands clapped down on my hips with an iron grip, holding me so I straddled him.

"No mating..." Vargan muttered, mostly to himself, forcing himself to let me go. I slid into the space between him and Ghain, both of their cocks arcing hard and aching over their bellies.

"Mm..." I let out a little sigh of pleasure as I wrapped my hand around each of them, but Ghain was the more expressive. Vargan's reactions were muted, just little twitches of his facial muscle like the process hurt him. Ghain became putty in my hand—really, really thick throbbing putty that jerked and spewed pre-cum with glorious abandon.

But Ghain forced his eyes open, sucking in a few breaths before saying, "Turn around, my Lay-la."

"What?"

"He wants to touch you as you touch him," Kren said in a sleepy voice, watching the proceedings with heavily lidded eyes.

"Oh, he..."

I probably should have demurred and made this about him, but the deep ache inside me had me moving, sitting down on my calves, their hands sliding between my thighs the moment I had their cocks in my grasp again, which just made everything messy. Was I getting pleasure from their stroking fingers, fighting to wedge themselves inside me, to strum at my clit? Or was it the thrust of their cocks, that ever so enticing spicy scent drawing me up on my hands and knees to lick at the heads?

There didn't seem to be any point of differentiation. There was a fire inside me, and every thrusting finger, every stroke, every sucking swallow of cum just seemed to stoke it higher. We all worked together to wring every scrap of pleasure from the moment, Ghain dragging me over to sit on his face, grinding me down until I feared he couldn't breathe, at the same time as

Vargan rose up, cock in hand. I fought to swallow as much of Ghain as he worked to devour me and Vargan stroked his massive cock with a sharp brutality I wouldn't dare.

And just like that, my orgasm smashed into me sideways, forcing me to grind my cunt shamelessly into Ghain's face, his groans of pleasure only making me cry out, the sounds muffled by the thrust of his cock into my mouth. Just as with Kren, his cum flooded my mouth right as Vargan's splattered all over my skin. All that remained was bliss—pure, unadulterated, perfect bliss.

I collapsed down onto the bed surrounded by hard male bodies, Kren curling around my head at the base of the bed.

"This has been a terribly lazy day, my Lay-la," Vargan said as he ran his fingers through his seed, massaging it into my skin. "But I cannot bring myself to complain."

"By the Mothers, you wouldn't want to," Ghain shot back, his voice already drowsy. "If this is laziness, I want more of it. Much more."

"Later," I croaked out into the mattress. "Laila is broken right now."

"Then we will work hard to restore you when we wake," Kren promised.

Chapter 12

A sharp squawk had me jolting in bed, Ghain groaning and then vaulting out and onto the floor before walking towards the entrance. He was still splendidly naked, and I admit, my attention was captured by watching all that muscle move as he put up his fist, a crow landing on his forearm. He gave the bird some seeds from a jar by the doorway, and then, as it was busy, he unwrapped a small spiral of paper from around its legs.

Paper! My little artist heart beat excitedly.

"Who is sending us a bird?" Vargan asked with a groan, scrubbing his face as he sat up, but Kren, he remained sleepy and sweet, snuggling into me, breathing my scent in deep.

"Mahk," Ghain replied, looking troubled and then attempting to mask that. "We have permission to visit his territory."

"Mother has obviously been using her time wisely," Vargan said, getting out of bed and walking over to consult the piece of paper.

Apparently confident that Ghain had the message right, he pulled down a wooden box from a shelf and withdrew actual pencils. I was up and out of the bed, pulling on the undershirt I had been wearing before and coming over. I picked up one of the pencils, testing its blunt tip on my finger. Some sort of clay-slash-graphite pencil, it looked like. Vargan scribbled out a message, reattaching the paper in the small metal cuff around the bird's foot. After it had drunk some water as well, it flew off.

"We will travel to Mahk's tomorrow," Vargan said. "Leaving at first light."

"We'll take some of the honey Soo-zee likes so much," Ghain said. "And some of those stones."

"Agreed," Kren said. "Perhaps it will sweeten her some."

AND WITH THAT ominous statement in my mind, we set off as soon as day broke the next morning. Shoes had been fashioned for me out of leather, forming a kind of sandal of sorts. I was now trussed up in a shirt, an overdress, and a long furry shawl, which had been wrapped around me several times before we set out.

The land was beautiful. As we walked down the mountainside, we saw a thick layer of mist over the plains, making it look all soft and peaceful, but I wasn't about to be sucked in by that again. After the painted cat incident, I was on my guard, and so were the orcs. I was ringed by the three of them, their weapons carried loosely as we walked between the trees, but I caught the way their eyes scanned the forest. We came to the pathway that led to Judith's place but kept walking past it.

We were at it for several hours, and in that time, I saw so much more of the landscape here. A stunning waterfall with crisp, mineral tasting water and pale green stones that had been tumbled into soft round shapes. A dramatic ravine, our path taking us not close to the edge, but near enough to see the sharp drop-off. Old ruins, there seemed to be quite a lot of them scattered around the landscape. I wanted to stop and inspect the carvings inscribed on their sides, but I was urged on.

"We do not like having an unmated woman out in the

open," Ghain said. "It is too tempting for those who have never known the touch of a woman."

"I can see why," Kren said with a slow smile. "That thing you did with your mouth, Lay-la. I have never heard of anything of the like. It was…" He swallowed hard, his grin widening, his eyes becoming more heavily lidded. "I can go into the Mothers' embrace now, a happy orc."

"My mother told me of such things," Vargan said. "But she said it was only for very special occasions, when an orc has distinguished himself. You honour us."

"Ah…it's not quite such a big deal where I'm from," I replied.

"The women do this often?" Ghain asked.

"Well, I think so. I can't exactly speak for all of womenkind, but it's not unusual."

"Your body is bounteous and you perform sorcery with your mouth," he replied. "How are you not mated?"

I'd been walking for most of the morning, keeping up with the guys, though I assumed they were slowing their pace for me. It was only now, I ran out of steam. If I thought hard enough, I could see the club, those guys, hear their douchey words. They were nobodies, literally no one to me, but it was what they symbolised that made me hurt.

"Orcs in your world, do they have a preference for certain body types in women?"

"What do you mean?" Kren asked with a frown. We'd all stopped now.

"Like, do you guys like small women or tall? Little tits or big?" I clapped my hands down on my chest. "Little tiny slips of girls, or women with meat on their bones?" I gripped my stomach, trying really hard to just feel it, acknowledge it, without hating on it.

"Men in your world, they sort through women like shiny stones?" Vargan asked, bristling. "They scorn the Mothers' gift?"

"If you mean they like some body types and not others, then yeah. Girls can have big tits, though maybe not as big as mine, but their body needs to be teeny weeny." I drew a picture in the air of a slight hourglass figure. "Some guys are OK with a big arse, but not as big as mine, and it has to be super smooth. No cellulite."

The three of them stared at me with frowns now.

"But a helluva lot of guys, they want girls to be very slim, little tits, little arse before they'll even go near them. They scope the women out and only approach those that fit their idea of what is beautiful, and that's never been me…"

My voice trailed away, my ability to objectively talk about this fading.

"I know other women that look like me that find their mates. Some are confident and sassy." I clicked my fingers through the air, trying to look fierce. "But others are like me."

"And what are you, my Lay-la?"

Vargan's voice was soft, so soft right now, and that just made this harder.

"I guess I get scared before I even talk to people." My eyes dropped down to the ground. "I think I know what they think, what they feel, and just when I try to convince myself I'm being paranoid, they prove me right. That's how I came to be here—I heard some guys saying crappy things about me, and I just lost my shit, stormed out of the club, and then…"

"You came here," Ghain said. "Where orcs know the value of the Mothers' gift. I do not want you to return to such a place, where you would be disrespected." The other orcs rumbled their agreement.

"That is why you came through the portal," Vargan said. "It is why you are here. The Mothers brought you to our world so you would be appreciated for who you are."

"People do, don't worry," I said, taking on my usual placatory tone. Most of my friends who had never experienced this kind of bullshit, firstly, struggled to believe my stories, and then secondly, much worse, began to feel pity for me. I didn't want or need pity. My eyes scanned the leaf litter, taking in the different shapes but not really seeing them. "There are a lot of people who care about me, who think I'm awesome, which is why I need to get back. It's just dudes I have issues with."

"Human men," Kren spat. "They have rocks instead of brains."

"On that we agree," I said with a chuckle.

"Then we will speak to Soo-zee and find a way to return to your world," Vargan said.

"That's the plan."

"And we will come through the portal with you."

"What?"

"And we will challenge any of these unworthy men who dare insult our Lay-la."

"Whoa, whoa, that is not the plan."

"If you can return to your home and your people, you have no reason to say no to first courting."

"No, but—"

"We will protect your cave, present gifts to your parents and your friends. We will earn our place by your side by proving we are not like these unworthy men."

"Guys, guys." I put my hand up placatingly. "This is all very sweet…"

"Sweet is good," Ghain announced. "I love sweet. You are very sweet." He pulled me close and wrapped an arm around me as he started strolling up the path again. "This is a good plan."

"A very good plan," the others agreed, steering me forward.

"No, no, no, not a good plan. Not a good plan at all."

"How can you say no to first courting then?" they insisted. "That will be our first courting gift!"

They didn't listen to me one little bit as they all planned it out, not realising what kind of screaming, crying hysteria the sight of three orcs arriving in suburban Australia would create, let alone the arrival of the inevitable government agencies and their invasive testing, a la *E.T.* But their increasingly grandiose schemes kept us occupied, right up until we reached Mahk and Susie's place.

An older orc was at the entrance to the cave, watching us approach with a grim expression, but he was soon joined by an older woman, her long greying hair wound up and on top of her head in a style that approximated the sixties beehive. She flicked at her overdress, which admittedly looked quite elegant on her slender form, fussing until she looked down at us. Her face fell, then hardened as she took the four of us in.

"We bring you gifts, Soo-zee, mate of Mahk," Ghain said, coming forward and dropping his head down as he held out a large glass jar of honey.

"Why thank you," she replied, her American accent apparent. Interesting.

"Come inside and be welcome," Mahk said in a low growl.

"So you're the girl that came from my world?" Susie asked without even a hello.

"If you mean Earth, then yeah."

"And you're what?" Her eyes narrowed, her brow creasing. "English?"

"Australian."

"Right, right. Well, you're a plump little thing, aren't you?" She looked me up and down, then turned on her heel. "I guess you better come in."

I felt, rather than saw, the moment my orcs stiffened, but they made the proper pleasantries as we entered the cave.

"So what can you tell me?" she asked brightly. "How the hell do I get out of this shithole?"

Chapter 13

This was not going to plan.

"Take a seat, take a seat," Susie said with a flick of her hand. "I'm Susie, and you are?"

"Laila."

"Laila. Cute name. So, what year is it now back home, 2000?"

"It's 2018," I replied, settling into a chair, two of my orcs doing the same, but Ghain came and sat on the floor by my feet. My fingers twitched with the need to rake through his ruffled hair.

"Damn, time has flown," Susie said, flopping down in a chair herself. "Mahk, be a dear and get our guests a drink." Mahk nodded and went to do just that. "I came through in sixty-nine. I was at Woodstock and took some really bad acid this guy gave me. Part of me wonders if I'm still tripping, locked up in some facility somewhere."

"Which guy?" I asked, seeing the hot barman for a moment and his acid green drink.

"He was hot," she said with a grin, not seeming to see Mahk's flinch as he distributed horns to everyone. I drank mine gratefully after the long walk. "Had light brown hair, crazy cheekbones, eyes that just smouldered, and—"

"A neat beard," I finished for her. She blinked, then sat up straight, really paying attention to me, because as her bright blue eyes met mine, I knew somehow, we'd met the same guy.

"And he gave you acid too?" she asked, all the arch confidence leaving her voice. "Is that what this is? Some kind of tapping into the collective unconscious? Because that is not cool."

"No, I was in a club and he made me a drink for free. It was really bright green."

"So was mine, the acid I mean. It was soaked into this blotter paper printed with all these green faces on it. I didn't pay too much attention. It was free and…" Susie shook her head. "I was having a great time, and then I woke up here."

"So it was a wizard that brought you to us," Vargan said.

"He is a creature of the Mothers," Kren added confidently. "He knew you were not being treated well by the human men, so he sent you here."

"Not treated well…?" Susie's face transformed into a vicious mask of scorn. "Honey, I was treated just fine. The guy who did me wrong was that wizard, the lousy bastard. I worked as an air hostess before I came here, jet-setting across the world and seeing, amazing things and then…" Her brows wrinkled until her hand rose absently to smooth them again. "And then I came here, where just getting to walk to the chieftain's place makes it a red-letter day."

She seemed to visibly deflate.

"Where did you come through?" I asked. "Have you ever been back there?"

"I was stoned outta my mind. Pretty sure I thought I was in an episode of *H.R. PufnStuf* for the first day. Then reality hit me. I wouldn't have the faintest idea." Then her eyes slid to me. "But you'd know, wouldn't you?"

"We can take you back to the place you entered this world,"

Vargan said. "Do you think we will find the portal there? We must bring gifts, so we can take them to your family."

I was going to have to break it to them gently, the impossibility of their plan, but I didn't get the chance. Susie's laughter was the bright airy sound of a total bitch. She laughed and laughed while everyone looked on, including Mahk, until finally, she brushed some tears away, struggling for composure.

"Is that what you fellas think you're gonna do? Go through the portal into our world?" Her voice dripped scorn, but she turned to Mahk. "I'm gonna need you to go with these guys, check it out."

"Of course, my Soo-zee."

"Damn, you'd think he'd get my name right after all these years, but nope," she said to me, as if none of the orcs could hear her. "If we found a portal back to Australia, I could call up some of my old airline buddies, get a ticket out of there and back home."

I understood my orcs' reticence now in bringing me to Susie. She was like a cat, caught up in its own instincts, cruel as they were, and unable to see past them. I looked up at Mahk and saw the face of a man that was quietly having his heart ripped in two, and Susie had no idea. I was sure he'd told her, but she'd have to have some compassion for that to register. Susie saw him as some kind of minion, at her beck and call, which made me wonder about their relationship.

Like my cave, the beds were in the main living area. Beds. One was quite large, the other almost an afterthought, and I was willing to bet I knew which one slept where. I felt a hot flush of rage rise inside me and knew then I needed to get the hell out of here.

"Is the place I stumbled through, is it close to here?" I asked my orcs.

"It's a few hours' walk, but we could make it there and back to the cave before dark, if you allowed us to carry you back," Vargan said.

That completely ignored the possibility that I might not be returning with them.

"Then let's do that," I said, getting to my feet. "Thanks, Susie, for letting us come by."

"Hey, not like I'm doing anything else here. Mahk, honey, can you mix me my medicine before you go? My head…"

Her hand fluttered dramatically as she put her fingers to her brow, and Mahk just grunted, using some of the honey we'd brought to pour into a bowl, then reached up and grabbed a container of powder he kept on a shelf too high for Susie to get to. Her eyes lit up with a curious light as he made the mixture. She sat forward in her chair, entirely alert as he came over with the bowl and a carved wooden spoon.

"Thanks, baby," she said in the first soft tone since we'd gotten here. She opened her mouth like a child and Mahk spooned the honey in. "Mmmm, that's the stuff." She flopped back onto the chair, her body going limp as she appeared to pass out.

"You can show me this place on the map?" Mahk said, speaking for the first time. Vargan nodded, getting to his feet, the two of them consulting a rolled up piece of vellum Mahk retrieved from deep in his cave. They discussed the site in detail before he nodded.

"If the portal is there, Mahk, you have to consider letting Soo-zee go through, back to her people. If she was a human born here, she would have been returned to the human villages, unfit to be an orc mate," Vargan said.

"You have cared for her for many years," Kren added. "But she gets no better."

"She needs more and more poppy milk," Ghain said. "Doesn't she?"

"My mate is my concern and none of yours," Mahk replied. "I will visit this site in a day or two and report back if I find anything."

The orcs nodded sadly, and I felt like they doubted he actually would, but we would. We filed out of the cave and said our goodbyes before going down the mountainside and back into the forest.

"Some women, they take some time to adjust to being an orc mate," Ghain said in a tentative tone. "They do not heed the Mothers' call, or are not able to appreciate their gifts. Sometimes poppy milk is used in the first few days, particularly if she has experienced pain at the hands of men. But it's always only for a short period of time and less and less each day. Except with Soo-zee."

"The apothecary who we go to for medicines does not want to sell any more milk to Mahk, but when she starts to wean off…" Kren shuddered.

"She should go home," Vargan said with a frown. "I do not question the Mothers' will often, but in this case?" He shook his head. "This is not the world for her."

"Nor is mine," I said. "If she came through in 1969? That was almost fifty years ago. She wouldn't recognise my world anymore. She needs to go to rehab if she's been taking heroin for that long."

"What is heroin, Lay-la? And what is rehab?"

WE TALKED MORE about my world than we had since I'd been found. They were suitably curious, but I could see some of their confidence waning. It should have. I hated that, but the reality was, my world was not the world for them. Of course, I wasn't in the driver's seat, making decisions. That was the role of the mysterious Mothers.

We walked and walked, until finally, we came to a section of the forest that, to me, seemed like anywhere else.

"This is it," Vargan said, looking around him. "We found you here."

"How can you tell?" I asked.

"The tree with the double forked branches was there," Ghain said, pointing to the one he was talking about. "The big boulder was there."

"And you came stumbling through those bushes," Kren said.

It was somewhat surreal, re-experiencing this, sober and in the daylight. The sun was getting lower in the sky, the air cooling, but it wasn't quite dusk yet. I walked over to the bushes as it all came back to me. I'd stumbled through the bushes then, but this time, I walked more carefully, bending down to pick up some coins and money that had obviously fallen from my pockets and stuffing them into my dress. They followed me, my guardians, allowing me to find the trail, and they joined me on it. It was darker here, under the shade of a massive tree, so that was what made the silvery back of my phone more stark. I dropped down to my knees, clearing away the leaves and picking it up.

"What is that, my Lay-la?" one of them asked, but I couldn't pay attention to that. Despite my fear of being just as fucking rude as Susie, I ignored them and tapped on my screen to wake it up.

Fifty-six percent battery, I thought with a sigh. Thank god I'd charged the thing before I left, but hope against hope, I checked the signal on my phone. I don't know why. I wasn't sure how I'd gotten here, but I'd moved past the point of not believing where I was, so it didn't make sense that there would be mobile phone reception. This wasn't some tiny little fragment of strangeness, somehow hidden on the Earth's surface. This place was called Lunor, it had three moons and no Optus towers. Yet as that reality hit home, something dropped inside me, my heart, my feeling of hope, I don't know what. I straightened up and turned to the guys.

"It's a mobile phone," I said. "It's kinda like…those birds you use. In my world, we would be able to contact other people using it. See?"

I opened my messages app, showing them the conversation I'd had with Hannah the night we left, and then was forced to step backwards as the orcs crowded in to take a look, which was a mistake. A small vibration in my hand, that was all it took to alert me that we were not entirely in Lunor anymore. Drums started up in my ears... Or was that my heartbeat as I wrenched the phone back toward me and stared at it?

Where R U!? Hannah's message shrieked, and then another and then another. They popped up over and over, and when I glanced up, I saw I had one measly bar of connectivity at the top of my phone. I wrenched the device back, using it now as a compass to take me back—back to where I was supposed to be. Another bar popped up, and then another, before the place between opened up.

I knew exactly where I was when I looked up, because it was so much louder. The steady thud of a heavy bass line, the screech of cars pulling past, the whisper of the wind, and the call of night birds. I looked up at the night sky, and sure enough, there was the single moon and the fucking Southern Cross. I'd done it. I'd found a way home.

So why did I feel a sudden stab in my chest? I turned back to the darkness, seeing the place between now as a shadow within a shadow, and my eyes ached. Vargan, Ghain, and Kren... I'd just walked out on them without even saying goodbye, being as big a bitch as Susie in the end. Why hadn't I waited, explained, given them some sort of closure?

Or given myself some.

Tears formed, for real now, and I brushed them away angrily. I'd been so focussed on finding my way home, I'd forgotten—

My maudlin thoughts were quickly interrupted by the sight of three massive orc warriors stepping through the portal.

Oh. My. God.

They were in a suburban park in Australia, looking like Peter Jackson's wet fucking dream.

Why the hell wasn't I born in New Zealand? I thought furiously, right before my legs gave out.

Chapter 14

"My Lay-la?"

I blinked furiously, and then when I saw the three orc men looking down at me, I let out a big sigh. It was all good. I was still in the orc realm, I was still being looked after by the guys. Then I heard the sound of some boy racer doing a burnout, and as I stiffened, so did they. I was scooped up and held against a chest as the other two both fell into an aggressive stance. Ghain, it was Ghain holding me.

"Guys?" I wiggled in Ghain's grip, but he just hugged me tighter. "Guys, seriously—"

"Ssh, Lay-La. There is something out there we do not recognise the sound of," Vargan said with all authority until I stopped thrashing and just let out a long sigh.

"I know exactly what it is, and if you'd just let me down—" I was placed on the ground seconds later. "Fuck, I don't know how to tell you this." The three of them turned to me. "You're in my realm. Look."

The orcs all gazed up at the sky, then swore as they saw the one moon.

"This is why the men here have fallen so far from the path. They only have the one Mother," Kren said.

"The moon is nothing more than a shiny rock here," I said, my head starting to really hurt. I rubbed at my temple as I continued, "We sent men up there to walk around on it."

The orcs balked at that, giving me the exact same look humans would when they caught sight of them.

"That is not possible," Ghain insisted.

"I can show you a video if you like," I said, tapping on my phone, and that was when Hannah's call came through.

"*Jesus, Laila! Where the hell are you? I've been in the loos, in the bar, asked the barmen, and the door dude said you stumbled out and took your shoes off!*"

OK, so apparently, no time had passed since I left.

"Hannah, I'm really sorry. I had a…thing. Look, there's a park just across the road from the club."

"*What? Why the hell are you in a park?*"

"Just…come outside, will you? I'll direct you to where we are."

"*We?*" I heard the muffled sound of the club as she obviously took my direction, and sure enough, there she was, standing on the footpath outside the club.

"I can see you," I said. "Just cross the road and then walk straight, OK?"

She did just that, and as I watched her look both ways, pausing for a car to go past, my heart wrenched. I didn't want to come back home for my phone or Netflix or even my books. This was what I'd wanted. There were people I cared about here, and yet, as I looked over my shoulder, I realised that there were people I cared about in Lunor too. I was stuck in the middle of two things all over again, without knowing what to do. I made myself focus as Hannah came stumbling over, the grass not great for heels.

"Laila?" she called out, somewhat tentatively.

"Here." I stepped out from behind the bushes, a picture now,

I'm assuming, in my homespun frock rather than the dress she'd given me.

"Laila?" She squinted at me hard, taking every inch of me in, then taking a few steps forward, then stopping. "Oh shit…"

I watched her eyes rake upwards and knew the guys had come to stand behind me.

"Look, I can explain—"

"Yeah, you can. Those are fucking orcs. How the hell did you find three fucking orcs?"

"Is this woman a friend, Lay-la?" Vargan asked in a low growl, coming to stand beside me. "Or is she one of those teeny women the men disrespect you for not being?"

"Ahh, OK, so if we can all just calm down for a second," I said.

"Oookay, Laila. Look, I…um…I need to give Bruce a call," Hannah said, looking at me sideways, and it was now I realised how unsurprised she was acting. Like, beyond the initial 'oh shit,' there was no extended existential crisis like I'd had. She was matter-of-fact about it all, had a guy who could deal with this situation whose name was Bruce, and why the hell was that?

"Who's Bruce?" I asked, kinda dreading getting the answer to that.

"Oh, Bruce is—" Hannah started to say with a kind of studied casualness.

"This is not a woman," Kren said, looking at Hannah sideways. "This is an elf."

I chuckled at that. Well, I tried. It came out kinda unhinged and hysterical instead.

"This is Hannah," I explained with special care. For me, not them. It felt like reality itself had now become this soft, malleable thing, whereas formerly, it had been a fixed quality all my life. "We grew up together. She's my best friend."

"Aw, bestie!" she said, walking over and slinging an arm around me. "So I'll just make a call, and Bruce will find the jolly green giants here a place to stay and then we can head home. You gotta tell me how you found these guys."

Orc-ward Encounters

"Um...just wait." I waved my hand in the air, feeling that dizziness beginning to rise again. "Just one minute. You're not surprised orcs are in the park?"

She shrugged her shoulders. "It happens from time to time. All sorts of creatures from other realms stumble in. The faerie circles or thin places of legends, they're real. We used to police them back in the day, but couldn't do as good a job as we can now, what with technology and everything."

"And you're a what? An elf? And your job is to...police the thin places?"

She looked up at me, reaching up to push my hair back from my face.

"They won't let you remember this, so I guess I should just tell you." Her smile, when it came, was incredibly sad, but she took a big breath out, and then there they were—two gossamer fine wings. "I'm not an elf."

"Looks like an elf to me," Kren insisted.

"In my world, I'm high fae. I was a changeling, left with my family to care for, though I don't know if they swapped Mum and Dad's real baby for me." She shuddered. "Or I was just gifted to them and they were made to think they'd given birth to me. No one has ever said anything, no matter how many times I ask. I could always glamour people when I was a kid, make them want to give me what I wanted, make them pay attention to me. Everyone except you, Laila."

Hannah seemed lighter somehow, like everything she was saying was a burden she could now put down, if only for a few minutes.

"I had to work at getting you to like me, be a better person, and when I was, I found I was happier." She grabbed my hand and gave it a squeeze. "Being around you taught me how to be human." Then she shook her head slowly. "The Centre for Paranormal Control found me when I was a teenager and brought me in. Scared the bloody shit out of me, but they tested me, saw I was a benign influence on the community and that I could suppress my less human attributes." She fluttered her wings. "So when I got out of school, I got a job with them, helping hide the paranormals that came through and hopefully getting them home."

Her eyes flicked to the orcs.

"Like we'll do with you three big fellas."

"No, tiny elf woman," Vargan insisted. "We are here to demonstrate our worthiness to Lay-la's family and friends so she will agree to first courting."

"You may show us where her mother and father are, but that is all, elf," Kren added, hefting his axe in his hand as Hannah's eyes went wide.

"Oh no…" she said, a smirk spreading across her face. "You didn't, did you?" She searched my face, but the sheer look of glee there did not make me feel any better. "Where did these guys come from? What happened to you and the dress I gave you? And the makeup?"

"I've been in an alternate realm for nearly two days, and these guys want me as their mate." I blurted it all out, unable to finesse the story, and Hannah just laughed, staring at all four of us, wide-eyed.

"Oh, wait until Bruce hears about this."

Chapter 15

Bruce was apparently a really fucking big ogre. He pulled up in a van in the carpark adjoining the park and then ambled over. I just stared at his greyish green skin that had the texture of a mossy rock and his craggy features that were far from human.

"So what do we have here?" he said, eyeing the lot of us. He pulled out his phone and started taking some notes. "Three orc warriors. Where you from, mate?"

"Mate?" Ghain recoiled. "You are not our mate. We intend for Lay-la to be our mate."

"Buddy, pal," Bruce explained. "Word means something different here. So what is the place you're from called?"

"Lunor," I replied.

"Lunor?" His eyebrows shot up, but he took down the details anyway. "Don't get many from there. So what happened, pals? Found an ancient portal you shouldn't have been playing with and stumbled through here?"

"Ah no," I replied. Bruce looked down at me with a faint air of irritation. "I stumbled into their realm after I'd been drinking in the bar, and I found them. Then I found a way back just now, and the guys came with me."

"We are here to visit Lay-la's parents and prove we're worthy mates," Vargan said.

Bruce just stared for a moment, then shrugged.

"Whatever you say, pal. Can you show me where you came through?"

We walked him over to the site, the dark rip in reality still there. He took a few photos with his phone and then nodded.

"We'll have some of the fellas put a barricade around it, add some pretty ripe septic smells. It'll keep the humans away until we can fix it."

"Fix it?" I said. "Hang on, what if we need to go back?"

"We?"

Bruce and Hannah said the same thing at the same time, their focus on me.

"Well, they have to go back, don't they? What will happen to the orcs if they stay here?"

"Some humanoid creatures who are able to assimilate well are given the options of glamours and going about their business. There's a ton of them down on Monster Street."

"Monster Street?" I asked.

"Out at Werribee," Hannah explained. "A lot of us settled there because we can let go of our glamours some of the time and just be."

"It's not ideal," Bruce continued. "We prefer people to integrate, but paranormals insist on clustering together. It's not very Australian."

"And you…?" I asked.

"Eighth generation Australian ogre," he replied, thumping his chest. "My family came out here with the First Fleet. Figured they could go and get lost in the bush, but the Aboriginal paranormals weren't having a bar of that. We ended up jammed in Melbourne, using glamours to stay under the radar. But back to your issue here. If the orcs can go back through the portal now, they should. If they stay here, I have to take them in for processing. And creatures like this?"

Bruce looked the three warriors up and down with an evaluating eye.

"Can you see them cooking up a feed on the barbie, listening to Triple J's hottest 100 with the rest of the country? I don't think so, mate. Especially as they tend to be polyamorous."

"Reverse harem," I corrected. Yeah, I'd read a few of those books in my time, and then there was the anime.

"Whatever. You gonna be able to explain to the neighbours you married three blokes who're built like brick shit houses? I don't think so, love."

"What is this barbie? Is it a feat of arms, because we are more than able to meet such a challenge," Vargan insisted, pushing himself forward.

"Any challenge," Ghain agreed, moving to stand with him, but Kren, he just wrapped his arms around me, holding me tight, and that was when Hannah's eyes widened.

"Fuck, you let this go too long, Han," Bruce said to my friend. "When these bastards bond with a chick, they're nigh on impossible to shift."

"I only just found them," she said in a hushed tone. "Laila was in the orc realm for a few days."

"Yeah, well, that's long enough. Hope you didn't leave any technology in Lunor, missy. That shit causes problems," Bruce said to me, then switched his attention to the orcs. "The girl stays here, and if you're smart, you'll go back to Lunor and find yourself a woman there. It'd save me the paperwork."

"No!"

The orcs had growled that response as I knew they would, but me? My fingers went to my lips as I realised I'd snapped the exact same thing.

Bruce looked at the four of us with the kind of long-suffering expression of dads, school bus drivers, and kids' footy coaches everywhere. It was the 'are you fucking kidding me?' look one delivered without actually saying anything.

"There's something here," Hannah murmured in a tone of awe. She looked at us more intently. "There's a bond."

"Well, fuck. Looks like a trip out to the processing facility is in order after all," Bruce grumbled. "You sure about this? Because once I send the paperwork in, the wheels are in motion."

"What wheels?" Vargan demanded. "What is paperwork?"

"Yeah, this is gonna go so fucking smoothly," Bruce replied. "Look, buddy, you're in a world real bloody different to yours. Walking around with those fucking meat cleavers is a big no-no for one. A copper sees you with one of them, you'd be in the slammer within seconds, and then being cut up and experimented on by shitty humans not long afterwards."

It hurt me to see the orcs struggling so hard to follow, even more to see the confusion and the desperation there. Their hands clasped around their axe hafts, but the weapons wouldn't help them this time. There was no painted cat to kill, no Urzog to dissuade.

"Guys, the customs in my world are very different," I said, putting a hand on Kren's arm, then Vargan's, then Ghain's. Their axes slowly lowered. "There's so many people here, we rarely use weapons to solve disputes, and brandishing them gets you in trouble. But mostly, it's a problem because people don't know that there are creatures other than humans here, and all of our stories about that often have people killing those creatures to try and understand them. Maybe you should go back. You got me home. As Bruce said, you could find another woman—"

"No, my Lay-la, no."

Vargan's massive hands cupped around my cheeks, Ghain and Kren's hands going to my hair. They held me, stroked me, and my eyes fell closed as I felt the warmth coming from them.

"What would we need to do to stay with our Lay-la?" Vargan asked in a low voice. "We will do anything."

"Well, pal, you'll be jumping into that van with me and going out to Werribee, where we've got the processing centre. You'll stay there for a while, be tested to see if you can make it in the human world, and then go through the education program.

But the big thing is going to be whether or not we can glamour you. No one with green skin and tusks is going to walk around downtown Melbourne, they just aren't."

"There is no one here like us?" Ghain asked.

"There's a few. I'll reach out to the orc community and see what we can do. Maybe there's someone who's willing to come talk to you about it. So what's it gonna be, fellas?"

Hannah studied me closely, trying to get a read on me, obviously, as this was discussed. Her eyes narrowed slightly, and she drew closer, scanning the air between me and the orcs. Was she cataloguing all the points by which we connected, or was it something else?

"We go where Lay-la goes," the guys insisted, and somehow, something settled inside me as a result. It was wrong, I knew that. In their own world, they could go and be the strong, vital warriors they were, but in this world? The only place for warriors was in the military, maybe, or at those weird CrossFit gyms. But I couldn't see my orcs fighting insurgents or flipping truck tyres. If they stayed here, all that they were would fade, and what would be left? I thought of Susie and her beehive hairdo as Mahk supplied her with her 'medicine.'

"You should go back," I insisted.

"No."

"You'll be fucking miserable here," I snapped, the three orcs jumping at my harsh tone, but I felt like one of those kids in the cartoons, where they were forced to be cruel to the wild animal they'd rescued, just to get it to go back to the wild. "There's no mountains to climb, no caves to live in, and no painted cats to hunt."

"We don't care," Ghain rumbled. "There is only you."

"And what about Judith? And your parents?" I looked at Kren, then Ghain, as all three of them flinched, but they rallied quickly.

"Some orcs travel far and wide to find their mate. This is accepted," Kren replied in a quiet voice. "Judith has birds to send for help. Others will step in and care for her. This is the way of the Mothers. Finding your mate is our most important task." He swept his taloned fingers through my hair. "And we have found her."

For a moment, there was no sound, no city, nothing but me and these three orcs whose lives I'd blundered into but couldn't seem to pull myself out of.

"We have come to your world. We have helped you get home. We have proved ourselves to be reliable and faithful," Vargan said. "Please, Lay-la, let us begin first courting?"

And just like that, I had no arguments left to make. With a tiny sob, I threw myself at them blindly, and they scooped me up and wrapped me in their arms.

"Yes. Of course, I'm going to say yes. Yes."

"This will be final courting too, I promise this, our Lay-la. You will never want for another."

The scary thing is, they were probably right, but fuck, how the hell was that going to work? I got to think long and hard on that as we were loaded into the back of Bruce's truck, sitting on the hard bench seats as he drove us out to the processing centre.

I WATCHED the truck pull up to a high, razor wire fence, a guy stepping out and acknowledging Bruce before allowing the gate to open and let us in. We rumbled up to a massive gleaming silver warehouse that sported a CSIRO sign on the side.

"The government science agency acts as a front for us," Bruce explained as we got out. "In return, we let them have a play with any cadavers we end up with. So, welcome to your new home for the foreseeable future."

"Laila will need to go with them," Hannah insisted as Bruce began to bristle. "They're already bonded, and company policy is we don't separate the bonded until it can be determined whether it will have an adverse effect on either party."

"Fine," he said, then slammed the truck door and tromped on over to the side door of the warehouse.

"We said we would overcome any challenge to be with you, Lay-la," Vargan said. "And we will, together."

"Together," the other two agreed as we followed Bruce. I just wished I had their confidence.

Chapter 16

"So what do we have here?" A woman with a clipboard walked towards us and then stopped, blinking. "Orcs?"

"I am Vargan, son of Judith, and this is—"

"Whoa, whoa, big fella," the woman said, then turned to Bruce. "I thought you were bullshitting me?"

"Unfortunately, no, Brenda. This is Kren, Vargan, and Ghain, all orcs from Lunor. Came through a rift in a park outside a nightclub in the city. They're bonded, so you're gonna have to put them in one of the unused werewolf dens," Bruce instructed. "It's all in the file I sent you."

"Right, right, OK then," the woman, Brenda, said. "If I can get you to come this way?"

"Caves in your world are strange," Ghain said, eyeing the inside of the warehouse. "They stink like metal."

"We do use metal for a lot of things," I said, but when I put my hand in his, he seemed to relax a little.

And brick and concrete and rubber—all things I was going to have to explain to the orcs. I let out a little sigh, seeing now what Bruce meant. He'd grown up in this world, been taught to hide what he was his whole life. I looked up at the guys and considered that. What would they do here? With their physiques, they'd be perfect for working on building sites or standing at the doors of clubs, working as bouncers, but was that what would make them happy? Those heavy thoughts trailed after me as I followed Brenda to our new digs.

A long howl cut through the air, making the orcs' hands go to their weapons, while Brenda went over and thumped on one of the cage walls.

"Keep it down, Ferris!" she snapped. "It's not even the full moon yet."

"These…werewolves," Vargan said cautiously. "They worship the moon?"

"Every damn night," she replied wearily.

"We are with the Mothers' people then," he said, nodding when the cage door was unlocked, opening into what was surprisingly a spacious suite.

"You've got separate bedrooms if you need them, or one big pack one if you like doing puppy piles." She pointed out the features of the room with a tip of her pen. "There's a communal bathroom and a kitchenette, but we provide food four times a day. Maybe more, depending on your individual constitution." Brenda eyed the orcs speculatively. "You're locked in, but that's as much for your own safety as anything. Once people get to know each other, start to get a feel for Earth, security is downgraded until you'll be let out into the community to live your own lives."

"This is dehumanising," I said, looking around the room. It wasn't awful, but…

"A helluva lot of immigration processes are, love," Brenda said before retrieving her swipe card to let herself out. "Get some sleep. We start things early in the morning. Someone will be by with your evening meal in a minute."

When she left, Hannah was still standing outside, her fingers pushed through the mesh of our cage.

"It won't be long, Laila, I promise. The orcs are intelligent. They'll be able to pick up the information needed quickly enough. Did you need me to fake a medical certificate for you to get some time off work?"

"Um, yes please." I looked down, then pushed my fingers through the mesh, just next to hers. "Does this mean they won't wipe my memory? That I'll remember…" I didn't specify what, but my eyes trailed over to take in her wings. They fluttered a little, and her smile grew a little misty.

"Yeah, I think you will." She blinked furiously. "I'm glad, for you, not me." She looked past me to the orcs. "Would I have chosen a trio of orcs for you? Probably not, but, Laila… They seem really into you. Like really, really, into you."

"We're going to try first courting, the precursor to becoming mates." I shrugged, suddenly feeling embarrassed by the idea, but she just squeaked with excitement.

"Oh my god, Laila! Orc husbands. Orc babies!"

Shit, I hadn't thought about that.

"They're so big and strong, and they'll keep you safe, treat you like you have always deserved."

"We will do better than the inferior men in this moonless world," Vargan insisted, coming over to stand by my side, and something inside me just uncoiled at the feel of his heavy hand on my shoulder. "They have not treated my Lay-la with proper respect."

Hannah's eyes went all shiny as she gazed up at him, then she giggled and bounced up and down.

"OMG, swoon! This is gonna be amazing, I know it. I'll see you on Monday, OK, and I'll sort things out with your work. Bye!"

I loved her optimism and it buoyed me up somewhat, but as she turned to go, the reality was that we were in a cage and she wasn't.

WE SAT DOWN and ate together when the food arrived. They seemed to understand orc preferences with trays of rare beef, seared vegetables, and containers of nuts. It was like a CrossFit dude's wet dream.

"What is this meat, my Lay-la?" Kren asked me as they tore into it with their belt knives.

"Beef. It comes from a cow. Here, I'll show you."

I brought up a picture on my phone and showed them what they looked like.

"Curious creatures," Vargan announced. "They look somewhat like the oxen the humans use to pull their carts, but this beef is satisfactory."

"That's called a steak." They looked at me blankly. "The cut of meat. It's from…" Shit, I didn't know which part of the cow a steak came from. The rump? "I think it's from this big muscle here. We have people whose job it is to carve up the dead cow into…"

In that moment, I could see the orcs working in a butcher's shop. With their knife skills and strength, they'd be slinging around cow carcasses like no one's business.

"Into what?"

"Steaks," I replied belatedly. "And other cuts of meat."

"I like this 'cut of meat,'" Ghain said. "It is tender and flavourful. We will command these people to bring us more steak."

I chuckled at that. "Well, if you like this, you're gonna love steak and blow jobs day."

It was an off the cuff joke, but the orcs went very, very still, and all of a sudden, their predatory natures came to the fore.

"A blow job is that delicious thing you did with your mouth?" Kren asked in a low, sinuous voice.

"Um, yeah. It's just a joke thing. It's like a special day for guys, but it's not a real thing. Well, mostly," I said, stiffening in my seat, but their relentlessly hot focus didn't shift.

"And what is this day for women?" Ghain asked, all innocent like.

"Chicken and lickin' day," I replied, going back to my meal.

"Send this steak back," Vargan announced, standing up, his

brethren by his side as he picked me up like a doll. "I have a hunger for this chicken."

"As do I," the others agreed.

I squirmed and protested right up until they found the pack room and I was tossed on top of a very big, very comfortable bed that made a king-sized one look like a matchbook. Then they silenced me by unclipping their leather arm bracers, their hands going to the ties of their loincloths.

"You were saying, my Lay-la?" Vargan asked with an arrogant smirk, and it was entirely justified. All that muscle on display and a whole lot more about to be revealed.

"We are conducting first courting, so we can't mate our Lay-la until she has decided," Kren said to the others.

What? No, no, no, no. Actually, I kinda babbled that, especially when loincloths were discarded and their hands dropped down to stroke their very big, very thick dicks. I followed the swivel of their palms like a participant being hypnotised at a carny show.

"But there is much we can do to persuade her," Ghain said with an evil grin. He fell down onto the bed, crawling towards me like some monster who was about to eat me all up, although I couldn't seem to find the energy to complain. The door to the room was kicked shut to give us some privacy, and then I shoved my hand in Ghain's hair and kissed his lips.

"Mm…" He let out appreciative little noises before pulling away and offering me to his brothers in arms. "This is the kissing thing our mothers spoke of. They did not mention how nice it is."

"I would like to try that," Vargan said, looming over me, soon joined by Kren.

"As would I."

And so I was dragged into the centre of the bed and passed from one orc to the other, until my lips felt twice as big from all the kisses.

"There is a condition of first courting we did not explain yet, Lay-la," Vargan said as I lay there in a daze. His fingers pushed up under the hem of my dress. "We do not wear clothing to bed." His dark eyes became serious, and I stared back, sensing the change in mood. "There can be nothing between us, not physical or emotional. We must be as naked as the first orcs and the first women were under the Mothers' light."

I was helped out of my clothes until I was exactly as they were, naked as the day I was born, while that same instinct to cover myself, protect my poor body from the gazes of others, rose and was set aside. They chose me, I had to remember that. They saw all I was and chose it. So when the orcs took my hands and placed them firmly on the bed, I let them, and then they went to work.

We have to make this work, I thought as I felt their kisses all over my skin. *I don't know what I'll do if it doesn't.*

Chapter 17

I was in heaven.

Ghain had pulled me back against his chest, but I was splayed out like a starfish as he played with my breasts, seeming to take inordinate satisfaction in teasing one nipple to an aching point, then the other, until I was gasping.

"This pleases you?" Kren asked. "Your thighs spread wider and then grow slick with your honey."

"Ah, yeah…" I gasped out. "It feels…" I let out a little moan as Ghain nibbled at my neck, rolling a nipple between his fingertips. "It feels like he's touching my clit at the same time."

"This is your Mothers' pearl?" Vargan asked, nudging the hood of my clit with a claw. "This is the source of your pleasure."

"One…"

I panted as a sharp bolt of pleasure shot through me. Somehow, their inspection, their questions, and Ghain's persistent caresses were driving me nuts. Or maybe it was because they were so unstudied. They wanted to learn everything about me so they might pleasure me for the rest of my life. I sucked in one breath, then another, feeling fear, pleasure, pain,

Orc-ward Encounters

but mostly need. I wanted that so very much, and I wanted them.

"One of them," I finally ground out.

"The place inside her," Kren said, then nipped at his talons to make sure they were blunt.

"Oh fuck…" I hissed as he pushed them inside me, somehow seeming to know exactly where to push up. His come-hither motion was going to have me hithering all too soon if he kept that up.

"And here." Vargan trailed his talons down my inner thighs, and for some reason, that made me shiver. "The Mothers' pearl has its roots deep in our Lay-la."

I didn't even know what that meant right now, but I knew how it felt. All their attention made my body feel like it had been lit on fire, and I knew exactly what I needed to put it out. Conscious, rational, non horny Laila knew that taking things to the next level right now was not smart, but horny Laila? I glanced down at those huge bobbing cocks and knew what I needed. A little whine of need escaped me, my hands reaching out, but they were moved away.

"You test our resolve," Vargan rumbled.

"Test it," I agreed frantically. "Let's test it."

"We madden our little human," Kren said with an evil smile, pulling out his fingers and then pushing them and another in.

"Jesus, that feels so bloody good…" I groaned. "But you would feel so much better."

"You are not ready, my Lay-la," Vargan insisted in a stern voice, but that just made me feel crazier. "We cannot rush first courting."

"So maybe don't get me so fucking horny," I shot back, pulling away from the two of them, then turning around to stare down at Ghain.

He looked like a deer in the headlights, but that suited me just fine. I straddled his hips, right as the others began to growl, and then slid my wet pussy up his swollen length. He let out some incomprehensible sound, right as his hands slapped down on my hips. I bent down, kissing him as my body moved, his own thrusts matching mine.

"Does that feel good?" I asked between kisses.

"So, so good…" Ghain ground out.

"What about this?"

I wriggled until I could feel the head of his cock partially notching against the mouth of my cunt. Ghain's eyes went wide as he felt my body suck at his, as if I needed him inside me, and I did. I was aching from all this foreplay, needing the real thing.

"My beautiful one, this is first courting. This is what it means," Vargan said, slipping behind me, his hands going over my breasts as I rutted against Ghain's prone form. "It creates a fire in our blood, forcing our needs to become pressing. That is the challenge of it. To find our way towards each other, right as our bodies scream for completion. Ghain wants nothing more than to bury himself in your tight little pleasure channel, doesn't he?"

The orc in question nodded furiously.

"But your body is not ready to accept us. Douse the fire together, and we will do so all through the night, filling you with our fingers and our tongues until you cannot take any more, but when you wake…" Vargan's claws stroked my nipples with an almost sinister intent. "You will not find yourself in great pain."

"Douse fire," I agreed mindlessly, grinding harder into Ghain, both our moans filling the room. "Stay unmated."

"For now…"

There was a dark promise in Vargan's words, but that was lost as Ghain and I began to move in earnest. Stroke for stroke now, I felt that thick cock slide along my seam, dragging sensually on my clit with every pass. My hands slapped down on the wall, kisses were rained down along my spine as we moved faster and faster, until our strokes, our breaths, shattered into desperate little spasms.

I felt Ghain's cum surge through his cock, triggering my own orgasm, the two of us sobbing out our pleasures until I collapsed

Orc-ward Encounters

down on top of him. Strong arms wrapped around me, holding me tight until he pulled away, staring into my eyes.

"You are so beautiful, my Lay-la," Ghain said.

"Don't say that." I went to pull away, to burrow my head in his shoulder, but he wouldn't let me pull away.

"Yes, say that. An orc walks the path of the Mothers. He speaks her truth," he replied.

"He speaks her truth," the other two intoned.

"My mother said that beauty is in the eye of the beholder, and in my eyes, you are the most beautiful." Ghain looked utterly earnest, his expression open and sweet in ways I didn't know if I'd ever seen, so I pressed my lips to his for a soft kiss. I couldn't see it at all, but I recognised that he did and maybe that was enough.

"And our beauty needs more before she is to sleep," Vargan ordered. "Clean up your mess and then relinquish our woman."

I thought he was going to find a spare T-shirt or whatever in the time-honoured postcoital tradition, but instead, Ghain lent down and licked me clean. When I started moaning again, that broad tongue seeming to hit every good spot I had, I was wrenched away.

"You always gorge yourself on the honey," Kren grumbled. "Save some for us."

"Oh, there's always more where that came from," I said airily as I was laid down on the bed. I was tired, my body loose, but as Kren settled down between my thighs, I felt the fire Vargan spoke of flaring harder again. His little catlike licks just seemed to exacerbate that, not resolve it. Then Vargan moved forward, straddling my shoulders with those massive thighs.

"We have had some steak," he said, looking down at me. "Is it time for blow jobs now?"

I watched the trickle of pre-cum slide down his thick shaft before licking up the centre to wipe it away.

"Yeah," I agreed. "I think it's time."

And when my lips fastened over his swollen head, I sucked down what felt like mouthfuls of the spicy sweet pre-cum they all seemed to make so readily as I stared up into his eyes. There was a dark promise there in Vargan's gaze, that he held on to for as long as he could, but we soon dissolved. The more frantic bobs of my head, the rapid flicker of Kren's tongue, they brought things roaring up and up, until we all burst together.

Vargan's hand cradled my head as he blasted my throat with his cum, right as Kren forced an almost screaming orgasm out of me. My body fought it, all of it, swallowing and thrashing and stiffening, until finally, Vargan withdrew his cock and I flopped down onto the bed, but we weren't finished. Kren jerked his cock, once, twice, three times, marking me so comprehensively as his, then the three of them smeared his seed all over my skin and massaged it in.

"We must rest," Vargan ordered in a hoarse voice. "The heat will rise again and again, and we must endure the testing they spoke of in the morning. Then more steak."

"And more blow jobs?" Ghain asked hopefully.

"Mm…" Kren replied. "I'm hoping chicken is on the menu tomorrow."

I was bundled up tightly between them, dropping into a sleep deeper and more satisfying than I had felt in a long time because this, this felt right in ways I'd never experienced. I just had to hang onto that feeling.

Chapter 18

So the next day was full of sex and protein, right? Alas, no. Before we could do anything about getting out of here, we needed to submit to a physical exam. Even me.

"This probably all seems a bit over the top," Doctor Angie told me. She'd introduced herself when I entered her consulting room, walking me over and giving me one of those green hospital gowns to put on. "You're human, you don't need testing," she said, as if I were making those protests. "But as you know, Australia takes quarantine very seriously. You might've picked up some bug or parasite while in Lunor—"

"Is that likely?" I asked, feeling trepidation rise.

"No, not likely, but we'll need to rule things out. So pop the gown on, and we'll take some tests. They aren't all that invasive, rest assured. Then the centre has asked me to talk to you about orc physiology."

"Orc physiology?"

My fingers froze around the gown as I stared at the doctor.

"Uh-huh. I'm assuming that you have not finalised the mating process with the band yet?"

"Ah, no."

"Good, good, then we've got time. So pop the gown on and…"

I was pinched, prodded, blood samples and swabs taken and put into little tubes for the pathology to run through their tests, but once I was dressed, I was forced to endure sex ed all over again. A diagram of a man's penis was projected up on the wall, and I just stared at it in confusion.

"So you obviously know how a man's penis works," the doctor said, using her clicker to change the image, now showing a dude with a boner. "When a man gets an erection, blood flow increases to his groin, creating the kind of tumescence required for sexual intercourse. Now an orc"—she clicked again, and the man boner shifted to the left, sitting there in comparison to the much more impressive orc boner—"is much the same, but for one crucial feature."

I swallowed hard, eyeing the two diagrams with increasing alarm.

"Before mating occurs, the orc's penis is much as a man's is, the only difference being in size, but when a woman agrees to take the band as her mate…"

She pressed on that clicker again. I really didn't need her to, but she did. The orc boner I had been used to seeing shifted to the left, booting the human one off the screen, and on the right…?

"What. The. Fuck?"

"Yes, well, that's why I've been asked to prepare you, because…"

Seminal vesicles. Swollen during mating. Wedged in at consummation. Locked inside. Her words washed over me, like waves of increasing roughness, until I was left gasping for breath.

"If we mate, I'll be forced to take that?"

I looked at the swollen protuberance at the base of the boner on the screen. It was a sullen lump, almost like a second set of testicles, and in some ways, it seemed to fulfil that purpose. Sperm pooled there in large amounts and was squeezed out into me as I came.

"There is no forcing in orc culture. Well, not from Lunor orcs," the doctor said. "There's no conception without female orgasm, so having respect and consideration for your partner is a key part of their culture's evolution. If you are concerned about being able to fit the knot in, I can put you onto some good toys that will help train your body to take it. There are some great sex toy companies that deal with anthropomorphic dildos, and there are also some BDSM places that sell inflatable ones that are probably more akin to what you'll face. So if you'd like me to put a list of appropriate devices together with some web links…?"

"I…" I put my hand up to stem the tide of words. "I just need you to stop talking about sex toys for a second."

"Of course. I'll give you a minute."

But a minute gave me time to gaze up at the diagram on the wall, come face-to-face with the medical reality of my future, and I wasn't sure it helped.

"If you can't go through with this," Doctor Angie said much more quietly, "I can find a way to get you out of the facility without having to face your suitors. For some girls, there's things that seem fine when they're stuck in an alternate realm, but when they come back…"

"No," I replied sharply, then again, much more definitely.

I could only imagine their faces if they were told I'd slunk out of the facility, leaving them here to what? Be sent back to Lunor? But it wasn't just about the pain it would cause them. I looked at the diagram in a different way now, a little cranky that the people here had decided to thrust the knowledge upon me so brusquely. I would've found this out anyway, and as I thought about it, Vargan's speech about being ready…

"I decided to go through first courting with the band," I said much more calmly. "And that's what I'm going to do. A woman's vagina can stretch enough for a baby to come out."

"That's certainly a more positive way of looking at it," the doctor said. "Well, just know if you are having any issues or doubts, the centre is here for you."

. . .

I EMERGED out into the hall, dressed again, to the sound of affronted shouts. I bustled over to find the band stumbling out of a consulting room, what looked like an ogre for a doctor coming out after them.

"If you want to stay here, you need to be tested!" he snapped.

"Guys, this is important," I said. They all went silent then, staring down at me. "We have rules in this country, and they must be followed. We need to run a few tests that won't hurt very much."

"He tried to touch my penis," Vargan rumbled.

I looked incredulously at the ogre.

"We need to rule out any sexually transmitted infections," the doctor said. "You have to agree, that's important."

"OK, it is," I agreed, and then was forced to go through an extensive discussion of what an STI was and then what bacteria and viruses were.

Fuck, this was hard, but they listened intently and as soon as it was made clear the potential threat there was to me and the community, they were cool. It didn't seem to hurt them, getting blood taken, but it was the invasion of their privacy they took issue with. They were damn lucky they weren't possessors of cervixes and needing regular pap smears. Then they had a sex education session too. The doctor offered me the opportunity to leave the room, but Kren grabbed me and hauled me up into his lap and held me close. Guess not then.

"OK, so you are aware that human women have a vagina?" the ogre said.

Censorious snorts from the orcs made that clear.

"Awesome, so let's talk through female physiology and the steps you'll need to take to ensure your bodies are compatible."

"Our mothers have already spoken of this," Vargan said. "They have schooled us well."

"Sure, we just want to be careful, for Laila's sake," the doctor said in his most reasonable tone. "Interspecies matings have been complicated in the past, and I've had to deal with women who have been hurt in the process." The guys' eyes swung my way. "We ogres have the same problem if we take mates of a small species. Women's vaginas can be very flexible, but it takes time to get them to a point of being able to accept a much larger penis, let alone one that knots."

"You mean our lock?" Ghain said, indicating the lump on the orc penis projected on the wall.

"Yes. Human men do not have such a thing."

"They truly are unworthy," Kren said, kissing the top of my head. "How on earth would that stimulate the Mothers' pearl of a woman from the inside when mating her?"

"Well, they can't," the doctor replied.

"It was definitely the Mothers' will that you come to us, Lay-la. When we mate, you will have everything you need."

OK, this was all getting really messy in my mind. On the one hand, the doctor was just advocating for me and doing so through some fairly clinical medical advice. On the other hand, I was learning a whole lot more about how orcs were prepared for sex with women, and as I felt Kren's massive arms pressing me against his body, that fire they said would never quite be put out was starting to rise from the ashes. To make things worse, Ghain slipped off the consulting table he was sitting on and went over to the vagina diagram on the wall.

"This is what we call the Mothers' pearl," he said to the doctor, somewhat patiently. "Its nub is here, but all of this is also sensitive." He ran a finger up and down the shaft of the clit you could barely see, making me shiver. "The roots of the pearl may also be felt here and here, depending on how deeply they are buried in a woman." He pointed to either side of the labia. "For us to mate with our Lay-la in the way of our fathers, we must prepare her for all of first courting. That means teasing her pleasure channel."

I jumped when his claws clacked against the screen at the mouth of the vagina.

"Working more and more of our fingers inside her."

"But slowly," Vargan added.

"Slowly, so that she comes to long for the stretch we will give her. This gives her time for the sensitive flesh around here" — Ghain circled the vaginal entrance— "to stretch to accommodate us. When our Lay-la chooses us, when she knows that we are in her heart as she is in ours, she will be able to take us and will crave our locks. It is only then that she will be ready. Our cum will be held tight in her body, her waves of pleasure sucking it deep inside her, where it will take root and we will have healthy orc sons to carry on our band's name."

The doctor interjected, discussed how long that might take and the concerns about vaginal trauma, but I couldn't seem to hear it. This was my sexual destiny laid out for me, and something inside me was one thousand percent on board. But it was Ghain's words, about me finding them in my heart, that was what grabbed at my attention the most. I wasn't there yet. We'd only been together a few days, but… An incredible tenderness flowered inside me, making my eyes ache, along with my heart.

"You are feeling needy, my Lay-la?" Kren asked me very quietly, whispering into my ear. I turned around, saw his eyes, and then Vargan's, shift to lock with mine.

"No," Vargan said with a shake of his head. "She begins to understand. This was a good conversation to have. Better than the 'testing.' Knowledge is always worth having, but we must get back to the den with our woman. We have always been taught to follow learning with application."

OK, definite shivers now. Really deep, really hot shivers.

"Fine," the ogre doctor said, throwing up his hands. "Classes won't begin until Monday anyway, but, Laila, are you all good with contraception? Things seem to be accelerating fast, and from experience, rational thought leaves the building when a heat comes on."

"Um, yeah, I've got the implant, but what is this heat thing?" I asked, feeling like I needed to shake my head to clear the heavy haze hanging over it.

"This is what I've been trying to talk to you about," the doctor said with a sigh. "Being with the orcs, being exposed to the pheromones of a band that you are drawn to, creates physiological changes in you. Greater relaxin production, that's the hormone that usually only rises during your period and pregnancy, but also there are shifts in your sexual responsiveness. You'll get turned on more easily and more often."

"Mm..." Kren let out a little grunt of satisfaction.

"Look, I'm teeing up the sick certificate for your workplace. Hannah gave us the details of where you work, but..." He pursed his lips. "I'd be prepared for an extensive leave of absence if I were you. We can't and won't keep you here against your will, but..." Kren's claws pricked at my skin as he held me tight.

"This is first courting," Vargan said. "There is no leaving, no going anywhere for our Lay-la."

His tone was deep and ominous, but that wasn't how my body responded. Some primal bitch part of me felt like she was being dragged back to the cave by her neanderthal hubby and she was down.

"We'll talk again when cooler heads prevail," the doc said, rising from his seat, towering over all of us.

Chapter 19

But there were no cooler heads around as we were escorted back to the den, the clang of the gate as it was shut and locked somehow comforting. Breakfast was already waiting for us, but no one seemed to pay that any mind as I was scooped up yet again and carried into the pack bedroom. My clothes were removed and so were theirs, and for a moment, I stopped them as they stood at the end of the bed. They stood so close as to be almost touching. I sat on the edge of the bed, and they were a wall of muscle before me. Part of me just wanted a moment, just one, to glory in the beauty that was before me, so I told them just that.

"We are yours," Ghain said, his voice low and husky. "You may do with us what you wilt."

So I did. I felt like a little girl let loose in a candy shop, my hands sliding across one hardened abdomen to another's taut hip, their muscles jumping at every caress, but that was just foreplay. My mouth watered as pre-cum spilled from their cocks, and I couldn't hold myself back. I sucked every drop from each one of them, the orcs groaning as more and more oozed free.

"We will spill and keep on spilling until there is no more to give," Vargan told me, gently pushing me backwards so I lay flat on the bed, but he dropped down to his knees between my open thighs. "We will always be hard, ready to give you our seed. It is you that needs tending and preparing."

For a moment, I saw that bulbous knot they called a lock, but suddenly, that made my cunt snap down tight, as if I could grip just that.

"You may suck my seed freely, if you wish," Ghain said, climbing onto the bed and coming to kneel by my head. "Our seed helps open you up, prepare you for what's coming."

I opened my mouth, and he fed his aching length inside, just the head, letting out a hiss as I lapped at the crown. Honey, sweet, sweet honey. I'd never be able to have it on crumpets without getting horny again.

"That's it," Kren crooned. "Suck down everything Ghain has to give you while I get better acquainted with these. Ach…"

The sound was a strangely harsh one, but Kren pressed his body to mine, lying on his side before covering my breast with his hand.

"The Mothers have truly blessed you, Lay-la," he said. I was forced to pull away from Ghain as his mouth sucked my nipple in. Vargan rumbled his approval as my thighs spread wider, his nails scoring my thighs. "Your body is as full and as beautiful as the moons themselves. I have not seen many human women blessed with breasts like yours."

"Yeah, that's why it's such a bastard to find a bra for them," I croaked out.

"That is that wretched corset thing you wear?" Ghain asked, then smiled darkly. "You will need not find any more, for we will serve in its place gladly."

"Spending my days carrying these?" Kren sucked one nipple, then the other, moving back and forth until my hips began to flex. "It is a task I will willingly undertake."

"Keep doing as you were, brother," Vargan instructed. "Her

pleasure channel flexes each time you suck." His teeth made short work of his claws, nipping them down to short and blunt, then tracing the edges of my cunt. "You must be able to take many of our fingers before we can conclude first mating. You may find us in your heart earlier, but we cannot proceed until, as your healer says, your body is ready. Suck Ghain's cock, take his seed down your throat. Take our 'pheromones' deep inside you and let them do their work."

Vargan's hand swept over my stomach possessively.

"The healer meant well, but we would never hurt you. The mothers taught all of us as young men how a woman must be cared for."

"Well, if you're sure," I said, flopping back on the bed.

I felt like I was being a bad sex partner. I was mostly lying back and letting them pleasure me as I suckled on Ghain, but their obvious pleasure in me doing just that gave me the permission I needed to be indulgent. I felt like I wanted to glut myself on the pleasure they gave me, this kind of pampering and surrender something few women in Australia right now would experience. So I gave in, humming around Ghain's cock as Kren teased and tweaked my nipples to the point of pain but not beyond it, then sucked away any discomfort, but it was Vargan that drove me mad. Gentle kisses pressed along with rounded tusks into my thighs, working his way up higher and higher until I just wanted to scream. Vargan chuckled, then uncurled that impressive tongue, separating my folds with the flat of it before slurping up everything he'd caught.

"You are ours," he promised darkly. "And your body begins to accept that. This is good."

Before I could think too long on that, he pushed two fingers inside me, but just the tips—enough to have me squirming for more. Ghain wouldn't relent, pushing his cock deeper into my mouth, flooding me with all that sweet pre-cum.

"Give her more, brother," he ground out. "She needs it."

"I want her screaming for it. It doesn't hurt to amplify our woman's need," Vargan said with a slow laugh.

"It will make her pleasure so much sharper, more thorough," Kren agreed, pricking just the points of his talons into my nipples. "Tease her more."

So Vargan did, circling the very areas where I needed him the most, my clit, my cunt twitching, but on what? He wouldn't touch me there apart from the most glancing of brushes. My hips jerked and shifted, trying to force the issue, but a strong hand on my pelvis pushed me down onto the bed and held me there. I was pinned by three horny orcs who seemed to have flipped the script at some point, going from sweet and accommodating to tortuous. Finally, I pulled my mouth free and stared at the three of them.

"Please? You're driving me fucking crazy here."

Their expressions softened instantly, but I was rewarded with a knowing shake of Vargan's head.

"You make it so hard to do what we need to, Lay-la. We know what's best."

I jolted off the bed as two fingers were slid inside me, pumping in and out. It felt like I could sense each knuckle. He pulled back and then tried to feed another in, but I instantly felt the pinch. Vargan moved up, coming to crouch between my legs, his cock in hand as he lowered his hips down.

"Shh shh…" Ghain said, stroking my hair. "He uses his honey to ease you."

"Oh shit, oh shit…" I yelped as the massive broad head was rubbed all over me, the hard versus slippery sensation driving me mad, but in his wake, my skin burned with pleasurable sensation, my nerve endings feeling like they'd only just come alive. I panted as Vargan anointed my clit, the sudden sensitisation washing over me. He stared down at me, smiling at me like I was the most beautiful thing in the world right now. "Oh my god." I stared at him, but nothing that was happening seemed a surprise for him. "Oh god!"

Orgasm can be like a wave that rises up and drowns us, but this was like a forest fire. It roared into life, my body dry tinder that was waiting to explode. As he rubbed against my clit, drenching it in his pre-cum, my whole body twitched and thrashed at the sensations that never really left.

"What the hell was that?" I gasped out, feeling like I was ready to come all over again, but Vargan moved his cock lower, making me groan as I felt it tease me open, just a little.

"You are starting to respond to our seed," Kren said, moving to his knees and then doing the same to my nipples, smearing his cock across them, leaving burning trails in his wake. "You are becoming ours. No other orc or man will be able to rouse you like this. You chose us, so we claim you. We must paint you with our seed, over and over, until you're ready."

"More?" Ghain asked, pressing his cock down, and I followed the slow drip of his cum with rapt fascination.

"More. Please, more."

I WAS FUCKING DELIRIOUS, sucking Ghain's cock harder and harder until his hips began to flex in time with my throat. Kren moved to straddle my chest, pushing my breasts together, fingers teasing the nipples as his cock slid between them. The room was filled with the sounds of our pleasure, but none more than mine.

Vargan was so meticulous, moving from my clit to my cunt and back again with his fingers, then brushing his cock against my folds to reapply his pre-cum when my skin lost some of this extra sensitivity. Then, at a moment I couldn't detect, he pushed his fingers in, stroking my G-spot with an assurance I'd never felt before. Slick oozed out of me, coating his fingers, something he praised over and over, especially when he could pull back and slip another finger in with greater ease. His fingers were so much thicker than the others, it was quite the feat, but that terrible tightness of feeling stretched around them gave me a pleasure I'd never really felt before. I hadn't known I was a size queen, but apparently, I was. I like to be filled to the brim and then some, that incredible fullness fulfilling a secret desire even I hadn't been willing to consider.

"You are doing so well, Lay-la," Vargan told me. "But I think you need to come now."

"Yes," Ghain and Kren groaned. "Now!"

Vargan kept up his punishing strokes inside me as Kren and Ghain rutted, my hand wrapping tight around the base of Ghain's cock, but it was Vargan's tongue and lips that undid me. They flickered against my clit, heralding the sure climb to orgasm, before he took it into his mouth and sucked.

I'm hoping you've had sexual experiences where you get everything you need. Every stroke, every minute or hour of glorious head, every inch of length or girth, because that was what I got now. My whole body lit up like Christmas lights, singing a primal song of pleasure, before ending on one long perfect note that even Mariah Carey couldn't hold.

As I came, Ghain's cock hardened and then shot cum down my throat, as Kren's sprayed all over my chest, and somehow, that just made it all better. Their pleasure was mine, and mine, theirs, until Kren fell off me and onto the bed and Vargan stepped up. He took his cock in hand, his strokes hypnotic as he pushed himself harder and harder, until finally, he erupted, this time angling his cock down. His cum splashed against my cunt, searing me.

I was done, so done, but as I floated off into afterglow, they all worked together, scooping up cum that had leaked and pushing it between my lips, massaging the seed on my breasts and between my legs into my skin until I was thoroughly marked.

"That will do for now," Vargan said with a satisfied nod. "But you will need frequent reapplications, my Lay-la."

"I don't think I can," I said on a groan. "I'm broken."

"Not broken," Ghain insisted, reaching down to kiss me. "Made anew."

"And now you must eat." Kren wrapped me up in a sheet like a Laila burrito and then carried me out of the room to the dining table, and this time, I didn't feel the need to protest. I was not capable of staggering out here.

"It is tempting to feed only one of your body's needs," Vargan observed. "But we must keep up our strength. First courting is the hardest challenge an orc may face."

Right now, I couldn't help but agree.

Chapter 20

And so it went for the rest of the day. I felt like I was always simmering in this hot, sensual haze, and then I'd find myself reaching for them, or curling within their arms and seeking their lips, then their cocks. They groaned with appreciation as I sucked one, then another dry, and whoever was left made sure I joined them in sexual fulfilment. I should have been aching, what with all the rubbing and teasing and doing every damn sexual act a group of four people can do without actual penile penetration, but there was something in that sweet cum of theirs. Friction and aching were things of the past, and there was only pleasure.

"I'm ready," I whined as Kren rubbed his cock all over my cunt. "I need you."

I reached up, hooking a hand around his neck and somehow able to wrestle him down, his heavy body pinning mine. His eyes went wide at this change in position, at the way the head of his cock slid farther in.

"No, my brother," Vargan rumbled. "Not yet. Her silken depths beckon all of us to bury ourselves inside her, but if she is getting close to physically accepting us, we must begin to woo her emotionally."

THE BEDROOM DOOR was slammed open, and we were forced to scramble, finding clothes to join Vargan outside, catching him in the act of dismantling the cage door.

"Whoa, whoa, big fella," Brenda said, some kind of elephant-sized stun gun in her hands, a group of other people running to the corridor toting much the same looking weapons.

"Our Lay-la has accepted the first stage of first courting. We must begin the next," Vargan announced, naked as a baby. A really, *really*, big baby.

"OK, and what's that when it's at home?" Brenda asked in a tight tone.

"We must show her the depths of our love for her so she can find us in her heart."

"Happy to help out there, big guy, but that can't entail walking around outside of the facility. You're too big, have no idea what's out there, and we haven't tried to put a glamour on any of you yet."

"Then we must inspect the facilities we can enter and find what we need here."

"Yeah?" Brenda lowered her gun and then the others did the same at her wave. "If you're willing to work with us, we're happy to help. We've all been there, trying to find a way to love in the human world. If you come with me, I'm happy to show you around. Just maybe put on some pants or something?"

"This is satisfactory. I will retrieve my loincloth. Wait here," Vargan said. As he re-entered the cage, he looked the three of us over. "One of you will need to remain and guard our Lay-la. The other beings here think the den is safe, but we cannot be too careful." He stopped and ran his knuckles down my cheek. "She is precious to us, so she will be to others."

"I'll stay," Ghain said with a grin, and the other two sniffed at that.

"You always shirk your duties," Kren grumbled.

"Ghain has nominated himself first, so he will stay," Vargan agreed, then he turned to me. "We will return soon with ways to show you what you mean to us. Lie in the arms of this laggard, Ghain, and try not to judge us by his sloth."

"I had not intended to lie about doing nothing," Ghain shot back. He nuzzled his head into mine so I twisted until my arms wrapped around his neck. "I can think of many worthy things to do with our mate."

"Well, no licking of her honey. You always gorge yourself on the sweet things," Kren said.

GHAIN AND I found ways to divert ourselves, looking through the photos on my phone, waiting for the others returned.

"The little elf is in many of your photos," Ghain observed. "We must prove to her that we are worthy of being your mates as well, then."

"Hannah's my best friend," I replied. "But you don't have to prove anything. Mostly, my family and Han, they just want someone who'll love me and stick by me."

"Well, that is easily done." Ghain's voice was much softer now, and when I turned to look up at him, he stroked his finger down the side of my face. "I thank the Mothers for watching over you and sending you our way. We wondered for some time if we would ever find a woman who would want us."

"You found it hard?" I asked with a small frown. "There were others before me?"

"No, but we put ourselves forward at the feasts where women made their choices, just like all the other orcs, but they did not bless us. No matter how big and strong we were, they overlooked us in favour of others. We attended over and over, each time hopeful, then disappointed. It became a chore, one we had to steel ourselves for. Vargan grew weary, Kren started to lose hope."

I blinked, finding it almost impossible to imagine the three of them putting themselves forward and a woman not choosing them. I was forced to endure the complicated feeling of anger on their behalf and relief on mine.

"And you?" I asked.

Ghain sighed and snuggled me in tighter against his chest.

"I just watched the moons and dreamed. It was that which brought us to you. I saw a dark shape cross the face of all three moons and assumed it was something, dragging the other two out into the night. I walked in the direction of the mysterious sign, and then we scented you."

He buried his face in my neck, the sensations making me giggle.

"Sweet as honey, it drew me near, and the others, they thought it was just me scenting a beehive again, but not this time. This was so much sweeter. We walked aimlessly around that forest until…"

I could see it just as clearly in my mind as he could. I'd stumbled out, drunk, and fallen at their feet.

"Laila, Ghain, it is time!"

We both jerked to attention as we heard the rest of the band arrive, but nothing prepared me for what we saw. Both orcs had slicked their long plaits back and tied them into neat ponytails, and each man now wore a button-up shirt and pants which must have come from the biggest and tallest menswear company in the country. They looked terribly uncomfortable, as well as earnest, as each clutched a handful of daisies and wildflowers.

"We are told that the plucking of flowers and offering them to future mates is a custom here," Vargan said, thrusting the mass of them at me, Kren doing the same.

"Oh my goodness," I said. "Thank you so much. Now I need a vase for them."

"What is a vase?" Kren asked sharply. "They did not tell us about vases."

"Never mind," I said, banging around in the kitchenette cupboards, then pulling out a pot before filling it with water. "This will do." I worked hard to get them to sit upright in the container, not just float on top of the water, and then put them on the dining table. I stood back and surveyed our handiwork and said, "They're beautiful. Thank you."

"Ahh, I see the wisdom of this now," Kren said. "We offer you pretty things in homage to your beauty."

"These flowers are not fine enough," Vargan said, eyeing them critically. "We must source better ones."

For a second, I just smiled, at their chatter, at their misinterpretation of human rituals, at all of it. I'd felt like a fish out of water at the club with Hannah, but here? We were all flip-flopping around, gasping for something we knew we needed but couldn't find, but we were doing it together.

They'd told me to find them in my heart, not realising they were already there.

"Now, Ghain, put this clothing on. Bren-dah informed us this is formal wear here."

"Like ceremonial garb?" he asked, plucking at the pile of fabric with his claws.

"Kren will help you to put it on. We tried to do it ourselves…" It was odd to see Vargan flush for a change. "It did not end well. Kren will assist you."

"And what will I be doing?" I asked with a smile, tweaking the folds of my overdress.

Vargan put his arm out stiffly, then looked down.

"I will take you on a date."

SO OBVIOUSLY THE education program had informally begun, because Vargan lifted up a massive picnic basket crammed full of food and escorted us out of the cage. Brenda just nodded as we passed, then opened the backdoor that led out to a massive field.

"It's all fenced off, and there's very thick trees around the perimeter of the field," she assured me as we walked. "Plus, we electrified the fence. You're safe out here."

Kren and Ghain joined us not long afterwards, and outside,

under a grey Melbourne sky, I was struck at how easily Ghain might pass as human. The shorter haircut with the clothing, it was working, though, as I looked at Kren and Vargan's plaits, I didn't want them to cut them. The green skin and tusks though…

It was tempting to take the pleasure out of this moment, to be concerned about how this would all work out, but as Vargan escorted me on his arm, I didn't let it. There was a whole organisation designed to help paranormal creatures co-exist. I had to believe they would help us.

Just as they had now. I laughed when I saw a massive blanket spread out on the grass as Vargan led me over to it. The other two sank down, but Ghain looked around with a question in his eyes before doing the same.

"For you, milady," Kren said, holding out a flute of white wine that seemed dwarfed by his massive hands. He'd struggled a bit with the bottle, but together, he and Vargan had managed to get the cork out. I inclined my head and accepted it with thanks, but every eye was on me as I took a tentative sip. It was light, cold, and a quite sweet white wine.

"Ooh, that's lovely."

That response, that was what they needed, and the fact such massive males needed validation too kinda helped me to relax a little. Food and drinks were pulled out, the three of them discussing the contents in a rapid chatter, but it was when Ghain pushed a strawberry my way, greenery first, I saw I had to intervene.

"The food here is different than you're used to, right?"

"Very," Ghain agreed. "I don't think I've ever seen fruit this bright red."

"You eat it like this." I grasped the stalk and took a bite, my hand jerking up to collect the juice that dripped from it.

"Mm…" Kren said. "That looks like something I want to try. It is juicy, like our mate."

I grinned and picked one up, holding the stalk but resisted his attempts to take it from me. He was forced to lean in and bite the fruit from my fingers. All those fangs, I admit, they were kind of scary, but they would never be deployed against me, I realised, not unless I wanted him to. Kren stared into my eyes as he ate his berry, until the sweetness hit him.

"Mothers…" he hissed, pulling away and wiping at his lips with the back of his hand.

"What is it?" Ghain asked in concern.

"The berry, it is so sweet!"

Ghain instantly picked up two, chomping one, then another, his eyes rolling closed.

"Mothers, these taste like honey and berries and…" he rhapsodised.

"And our mate," Kren asserted, picking up another and offering it to me. He seemed to watch my every move as I bit into the red fruit and chewed.

"Providing food is very important to orcs," Vargan explained. "To watch our mate eat is very satisfying."

And by satisfying, he meant something else, something that involved a lot more naked time, so I got in the mood, plucking up a strawberry and offering it to Vargan. He was the solemn leader of the band, the one who made sure we were all looked after, so I liked looking after him. He parted his lips but I brushed the fruit against them, then jerked it away, something that had his eyes widening and then blinking at me.

Those dark depths twinkled, then his hand shot out, wrapping around my wrist and forcing the fruit back towards him, where his perfect white teeth chomped down on it. He chewed, then stopped, glancing at the others, who nodded with encouragement, finishing the strawberry before grabbing another and putting it between my fingers. His grip encouraged me to feed him another, so I did with a chuckle. We had a lot more food, but right now, we stared out into the late afternoon sun and just sighed.

"Bren-dah told us this is a picnic. It is a very pleasant way of providing for your mate," Kren said.

"It is lovely," I agreed, leaning back onto Vargan, who held me against his chest.

"We were told it is a human tradition in this world to get to know your mate first, find out what she likes and dislikes," he said. "What do you like and dislike?"

I snorted at the very literal translation of the advice.

"Likes? I like drawing and painting."

"This is what you call your representations of things using charcoal?" Kren asked. "You drew Ghain." He sounded a little huffy about that.

"I did. I'd love to draw all of you, but all my art stuff is at home."

"This home…it is far from here?" Ghain asked.

"A few hours' drive, but not far. When I go back to work, I'll be down here at the end of every day, I promise," I said lightly, not thinking about how that would go over.

"Your work will take you away from us? You will walk out unmated in the world? Even with your unworthy men, I do not like this idea at all." I felt Vargan stiffen behind me, his arm biting into my middle as he got more roused. "Why must you work, Lay-la?"

"So in your world, you would go out and find food and hunt animals for their pelts, right?" They agreed. "Well in mine, you go to work so you might earn coins so you can buy the things you need."

"The humans do that in our world too," Ghain said to the others. "But the women usually stay back and care for the home."

"We were the same for a long time," I agreed, and they let out a collective sigh. "But feminism changed all of that. Women work, and it's everyone's job to care for children and the home."

There was a low hiss in response to this.

"My Lay-la…" Ghain's words were as tentative as an orc's could be. "Our tradition teaches us that meaningful lives come from tending to our mate and any children that we may be blessed with. That begins with first courting, and if you accept us, that continues until the Mothers take us back into their embrace. We would not be happy going to separate places to work. We want…"

"We want to work together," Kren said, and there was a slightly hurt edge to his voice that had me pushing away from Vargan and over to him. I lifted his head with my finger until he was forced to look at me. "We want to be together, always."

"Won't we be?" I replied. "If I become your mate, won't you be in my heart always, just like I'll be in yours?" He wrapped me in his arms and held me, burying his nose in my hair. "Humans in my world expect to spend time away from their family. If they're with them all the time, we tend to think they are being codependent."

"Codependent," he said. "Yes, I like that. Let's be codependent."

WE SAT and ate for some time, and I introduced them to a lot of cuisine from around the world. From feta cheese to sauerkraut, they inhaled the lot of it, trying to hassle me into trying the stuff I didn't want, but I redirected their attention to each other. It was a lovely date, and when we got back to the den, they removed the 'formal clothing' with a gratitude I understood well, but that didn't quiet the niggling in the back of my mind.

I don't know how I thought this was going to work. I was only just getting my head around the possibility of trying to, but I realised that this wasn't going to just come together without some effort on my part. I understood this world and how it worked, just as they had back in Lunor, and like them, I needed to do the work to help us find our place in it.

Chapter 21

Hannah turned up the next day for her work, which was apparently starting to help us.

"I've always worked as a paranormal liaison, helping people find their feet in the human world," she explained as she walked in, wheeling a familiar suitcase and toting a tray of lattes. "So as a result, I have your clothes, all your art gear from your place, and coffee."

"OMG, gimme!" I said, but moved over to give her a hug as she came into the den. "Thank you so much! It feels like ten thousand years and waiting since I've had a damn coffee." She handed me mine, and I took a grateful sip, trying very hard not to perform Snoopy's happy dance in response.

"What is kawfee?" Vargan asked, his eyes flicking between the two of us.

"Something you are going to become very familiar with, my friend, if you want to romance my Laila." She held out a disposable cup of it to him.

The three of them sniffed it warily, then Vargan tipped the cup up—

"Um, Vargan!"

—and down his throat.

"Bleurgh!"

Precious coffee splattered against the floor, and I fought the urge to cry. These were lattes made by this amazing old Italian guy in Fitzroy, and they'd just… The others took the lid off and poked their fingers into the liquid, licking the end, then recoiling in disgust.

"What is this stuff?" Kren asked.

"Do you have anything you drink to give you extra energy and stop you from feeling tired?" I asked.

"Ohh," Ghain said. "You mean like the seeds from the tree with the red leaves. We chew them when we go into battle, but—"

"Distasteful things," Kren agreed. "What battle do you prepare for, because we will fight for your honour. You have no need to drink this swill."

"I like drinking this gift from the gods themselves," I said, gripping my cup tighter.

"OK, Laila, calm down. The nice orc boys are not trying to take your precious coffee from you," Hannah said in a fake placating tone. "So today is the first day of assimilation school. You'll be learning all about the human world with Brenda and her team."

We turned around to see the woman herself was standing there, waving.

"Didn't rate those shirts, hey fellas?" she said.

The orcs had left on the dress pants, but nothing else. They were bare chested and bare footed and looking deliciously savage as a result.

"The pants are acceptable, but shirts? They are women's clothing, not those of warriors," Vargan insisted.

"Maybe, but we don't have a lot of need for warriors in Australia," Brenda said, and there was a slight air of sadness about her.

She knew what I did—these magnificent orcs would lose something if they were going to stay here. Our cultures and our lives were so different, there was no way around that. I would've had to do the same if I'd stayed in Lunor, never again picking up a Posca paint marker or a water-soluble oil pastel. The orcs insisted the Mothers were the ones that had brought us together, but I wasn't sure we were done realising the price of that. With that pensive thought, I wheeled my suitcase into the bedroom and got changed.

"IS EVERYTHING OK?" Hannah asked, sticking her head around the door once I was done. I zipped up my hoodie, the familiar feeling of comfort that came from wearing my favourite clothes settling me somewhat.

"Kind of. Can we get out of here today?"

"Um…sure. Where did you want to go?"

Home. The park. Somewhere familiar. The same old options rolled through my mind, but I reached for a new one.

"The guys are gonna be caught up in class all day, and I'm just going to spend the time fretting. You said there's paranormals already living out in the world, like you do."

"Yeah." She smiled slowly. "You need to see people who've done it successfully."

"Yeah." I nodded. "I think I do."

THE GUYS WEREN'T keen on me leaving without them, but a quick display of Hannah's powers seemed to assure them that she could take care of me.

"I've been looking after Laila for some time," she said. "You can trust me to keep on doing that."

They had their doubts, I could see it in the way they sought to size Hannah up, mistaking her size for her power. She zapped Vargan on the nose with some kind of twinkly blast, which had him clawing at his face.

"Stay with the tiny elf woman," Kren said, putting his massive hands on my shoulders. "If we must stay here…"

He wanted me to contradict that, to tell him he could come, that the band could follow me on whatever adventure I was about to go on, but I couldn't. The very things I loved about them were the things that made that impossible. I stroked my hand down his lean cheeks, tracing the little lines of scars that had been cut into his cheekbones as his eyes fell closed. There was something quiet, timeless, eternal about this, because it could be.

I could be stroking his cheeks as his skin began to wrinkle, as mine did, until our hair had turned grey, the strength in our arms finally failing—until the end. But for that to be a possibility, we each had our roles. They had to learn about the brand-new world they were in, and I had to find a place for them in it that wouldn't eat away everything they were until there was nothing left. I wrapped my arms around his neck, his going around me and holding me close, just being in this moment until the others decided to horn in. I chuckled, then relaxed as I felt the weight of all their bodies pressed against me.

Hannah's eyes shone when they finally let me go, Brenda smiling as she led them down the hallway to the classrooms.

"Oh my god…" Hannah said as they disappeared from sight. "This is real. It's only been a couple of days, but…"

"I know." I shrugged, shoving my hands deeper into the kangaroo pocket on my hoodie. "I don't know how, but it is."

"I was going to take you to meet one of the few orc families in town, figuring that might help, but I think I know where we need to go."

"Where?"

"Monster Street."

Chapter 22

We got into her car, and then things got a little weird. You know how in some cop dramas, when the detective pulls out a siren and slaps it on top of his unmarked car? Well, my best friend in the whole world did that, but instead of a siren, it was a massive spiky chunk of clear crystal and it was placed on top of the dash.

"What the hell is that?" I asked.

"Monster Street…" She chewed her lip as we drove out of the facility, past the tall gates and out onto the road. "You know Diagon Alley?"

"God yes! I wanted to go there so damn hard."

"I know," she said with a snort. "You were rabbiting on and on about wishing magic was real—"

"And it was for you." I stared at her, feeling a pang. "Jeez, Han, I must've been insufferable."

"No, not really." She smiled, then shot me a sidelong look. "If anything, it gave me hope. For a while there, we really thought that maybe books like *Harry Potter* might create more acceptance in the community of paranormal beings…but anyway, Monster Street. It's the place that paranormals who can't be assimilated into everyday society go, and just like Diagon Alley, it's not somewhere you can just stumble into."

She drove up the road, towards what looked like the main drag of the suburb, more and more commercial properties popping up, but as we got closer, the crystal began to glow with an unearthly iridescent blue light. I watched it not the road, so I didn't really see what happened properly, but when it flared a blinding electric blue, it was like the road in front of us separated, two pages parting to reveal a whole other one.

My face was plastered to the passenger seat window, staring as I tried to take it all in. Tall buildings that looked a lot like old Federation style terrace houses lined the road, shops down the bottom, residential at the top, but it wasn't just that. Though each one was painted an array of dizzying colours, it was the people that drew my eye.

A tall wolfen creature strolled down the street, and not the Jacob Black type. This was a bipedal wolf man walking on by, his hands shoved into the pockets of his jeans, a cigarette hanging out the side of his mouth. A long twisty dragon of the type seen in Chinese art flew past, spiralling through the air like one of those amazing kites. A fluttery fae woman with the wings of a monarch butterfly nodded to the wolf man as he watched her pass, leering at her arse, but the twitch of her antennae suggested she knew. A few massive minotaur men called out to her from across the street, but she just stalked on by.

"Oh my god…" I hissed. "Oh my god!"

"So, I'm gonna need you to find whatever chill you can, because tourists? They aren't looked upon kindly. These are people that have been relegated here, often through no fault of their own. They can't hold a glamour or resent having to. Or they stumbled through cracks in their world and into ours and couldn't find a way home. Or their kind existed here for some time and they needed to find a place to hide as the spread of humans took away all of the empty territories. Or they came through, thinking things would be better, and it was, sort of…"

She flicked me an apologetic look.

"And this is where you think we may end up," I said, looking at the street in a whole new way.

"It may." She pulled into a carpark, putting the brake on before turning in her seat to me. "You wanted to see what life might be like for you and your band of orcs. Well, this is it. They're so tall and muscular, and from what I've read about Lunorian society, there's such a gap in social norms and technology, they may not be able to make it in the real world. So…"

"So…" I echoed her, looking out through the windshield. The colours, the shops, the people walking past… It was all a bit different when it was potentially going to become our whole world. I blinked, seeing the wild orc lands, then Monster Street overlaid on top of each other, but my fingers wrapped around the door handle, wrenching the car door open, and I forced myself to step out and take a look.

You know when you go to the markets and there's like a million people jammed in the aisles, and as you shuffle past, you smell the scents of global cuisines cooking and meshing into one wildly clashing, sensory carpet? In some ways, that was what this was like.

"Laila? Laila!"

I heard Hannah calling my name, but I drifted up the footpath, peering inside the shop windows as I got closer. The first was a hair salon full of clients, all very normal. But it was the wolf girl getting a full body blow dry, standing on a podium that drew my eye, then a naga girl with a full head of luscious black hair getting a trim, her massive snake coils spilling beyond the confines of her chair. A dryad-looking woman was getting her branches trimmed by a chatty butterfly winged fae hairdresser sporting a pair of gardening shears. A massive troll woman looked kinda like a cluster of rocks until she moved, a buffing head attached to an angle grinder used by the attendant to shine up her skin. Slowly but surely, their eyes slid my way, of course they did, accompanied by small frowns. I was standing there like a Gumby, rudely fucking staring.

"Fuck, Laila!" Hannah said, grabbing on my arm and hauling me down the street. "You can't just go around staring like that. Get some chill, remember?"

"Yeah, I know, sorry." I wiped my hand across my face. "I'm just… I'm still getting my head around this all, y'know? Like, the guys, you, the Paranormal Centre…"

She patted my arm reassuringly.

"If it makes you feel any better, you're adjusting superfast. I've known people to still be in the total brainfart stage weeks after they find out." She pursed her lips and frowned. "They're the ones we usually mind wipe."

"Like…everything?" I asked tentatively.

"God, no. Just selective memory loss. Replace the memories of meeting a paranormal with something equally outlandish but much more credible. A kind of *Believe It or Not!* type of thing. Explains the deep feelings of surprise, but gives the brain something much more concrete to hang them on. They usually want that subconsciously by the time we step in."

She rubbed her hand up and down my arm.

"But that won't happen to you, so let's look at what your options are."

"HELLO, LADIES," an older man said, stepping out from his shop and onto the footpath with a well-practised smile. "Can I interest you in a statue to further beautify your homes? We can make anything of your choice in genuine Carrara marble, Pentelic, or beautiful Bianco Sivec."

"Are we ready, boys?" a confident young female said. We turned to see a girl with long dark hair and a heavy pair of black sunglasses on her eyes as she sauntered into the showroom, the two young men carrying in several pieces that looked like they were made of polystyrene models of Classical Greek or Roman statuary.

"Better look this way," the man said. "You're beautiful girls, but prettier breathing than as statues."

We quickly jerked our eyes away until we heard the girl say, "All right, all done. Call me when you need the next lot done." I turned around to see her sauntering back, her glasses firmly in place, though it was her hair that caught my eyes. Snakes... And those polystyrene mock-ups of statues? They were now shining marble renditions of the same thing, two in purest white marble, shot through with very faint threads of grey, though the last one was a deep black with white veins running through it. The boys had to work hard now to move each one individually, both working together to shift one sculpture slowly.

"My daughter, Themi, is a very powerful gorgon," the man explained. "Just like her mother, God rest her soul. Themi can control which stone she turns an item into, within reason. I had some of the dragons wanting junk turned into gold ore, but that's not possible, nor diamond. But if you want a marble piece that will beautify your home, Manoli's is the place to come. You want a *Venus de Milo* with arms? We can do you a deal, thirty percent off if you want the classic with no arms."

"Thanks, Manoli," I replied, "but I don't actually have a place to put statues in yet."

"You're moving into the street?" His dark eyebrow jerked up at that. "What brings you to the neighbourhood? You're not running with those minotaur boys across the road, are you?"

He directed our attention to where, indeed, there was a cluster of four young men standing around in skin-tight skinny leg jeans, expensive sneakers, and bare chests, each one sporting a rack of bullhorns at their temples. They were making a hell of a big noise, catcalling women as they walked past, getting in their faces before one of them changed her fingers into claws and raked them across his nose. He stumbled back, hands over his face, as the others howled with laughter.

"George is a good boy, but those others..." He shook his head definitely.

"Ah, no, I'm going through first courting with a band of orcs," I replied, feeling a little embarrassed as I did.

"First courting?" Manoli's eyes jerked back to me. "Lunorian or Solarian orcs?"

"Lunorian, but——"

"Well, that's OK then. The Solarian ones... That would not be a good match for a human woman. So where were you thinking of living...?"

"Laila," I replied.

"Laila. That's a pretty name. So were you thinking a house or an apartment, Laila? Because my brother-in-law, Michael, has a place on the outskirts of the street. Big block, nice house. Plenty of room for a growing family."

"Um...I don't know yet. It's early days, and my band are locked up in the centre for the moment."

"Just trying to get a feel for the neighbourhood then?" He shrugged. "Makes sense, but when you're ready, you come see me, right?"

"Um, yeah, sure."

"You lovely ladies have a good day."

He winked at us, then swung back into the shop, yelling instructions at the boys, critiquing the way they were carrying the statue.

"Well, he seemed nice," I said as we kept walking.

"People are, for the most part," Hannah said, smiling at me. "It's like any other neighbourhood."

EXCEPT A WHOLE LOT DIFFERENT.

We stopped to look through the window of the most stunning jewellery shop. It was boggle-the-mind amazing. Rings, necklaces, bracelets, groaning with precious and semi-precious stones, were heaped in the window in an almost careless display, and as you stared, you could see all the details more closely. Each piece was so ornate, with tiny decorations underlining and enhancing each element of the design.

Like this ring, which featured a big slab of turquoise. The stone had been shaped into an elongated teardrop shape, the matrix of the different shards of turquoise creating a textured focal point, but around the bezel were a million tiny little balls, then a twisted strand of silver, then an incised strip marked with symbols so small, you couldn't make them out. But even that wasn't all. Intricate shapes, that I think were minuscule little animals, had been carved into the thick ring, creating an even more complex piece.

"You should come and take a look if you're peering at that so closely," a gruff voice said. My eyes jerked sideways to see a small man with a full beard standing there with a cheeky smile. He was quite a bit shorter than me, yet despite his size, he hefted a huge box of stones and ores in his arms, the contents looking like it was easily twenty or thirty kilos. "The jeweller is a bit of a grouch." He winked at me. "But the other bloke who helps run the place is a pretty easy-going guy."

"What're you doing out there with them?" A sharp voice dragged our attention towards the doorway, where a massive, tall man stood. His blood was up, his skin flushed, his massive chest heaving as he looked the box of ores and stones over with a covetous eye. "Bring the pretties inside, quickly, quickly," he said, blinking, a transparent second eyelid covering his eyes momentarily.

"Hold your horses!" the smaller man said. "I was just talking to these nice ladies, seeing if they'd like to come and take a look. We need customers, Draco."

"No, we do not." Draco stared at the two of us flatly, inspecting our clothing, our general appearance, and dismissing us with a sniff. "We do not need to sell anything."

"Whole purpose of running a shop, mate," the smaller man shot back. "People buy jewellery, we get money."

"Money…" Draco said the word with a kind of sibilant hiss. "OK, they may come in."

"Um, we'll probably keep going," Hannah said, "but nice to meet…"

"Frag," the smaller man said, holding out a hand, and Hannah shook it. "Don't worry about Draco here. Dragon shifters, they work metal like a devil, but getting them to part with their creations…? So neither of you are in the market for a new piece? We've got some pretties inside that would look brilliant on either of you."

"For money," Draco added, narrowing his eyes.

"I think we're going to need to save our money for housing," I said, "so you get to keep your pretties a while longer, Draco."

The dragon shifter snorted at that, small plumes of smoke escaping his nostrils, before he turned on his heel and stalked back inside.

"You're looking to move out here?" Frag asked, and we gave him the same spiel. "Well, if you're looking to mate with a band of orcs, going to see Mama Rosa would be smart. Her band and their brood of unruly boys is down the street and off to your right."

"Thanks," we said, before walking down the road to follow his instructions, but as we went, we passed dozens of wild shops. Pet shops with creatures I had no name for, a florist shop where a dryad coaxed her blooms to grow in ways that pleased the buyer, and a whole foods shop, complete with big paper sacks of a multitude of exotic food and herbs, administered by some ethereal-looking elves wearing homespun linen clothes. But not all of Monster Street was going to be cool and groovy, we quickly found out.

In the way of bored young men everywhere, a bunch of orc lads hung around the front of a house with a modest front yard, loud music with a feral beat pumping from the speakers of a boom box as they talked shit, hung out, and practised their archery on a tree.

Wait, what?

I froze as I saw the next guy step up, raising his bow, the other boys catcalling and shouting stuff to try and throw him off his game, but he pulled the massive compound bow with little effort, his lips pressed against the string as he sighted the target down the arrow's shaft and then… *Thud!* Roars of appreciation went up through the group when the arrow buried itself in the tree trunk.

"So who do we have here?" the archer asked, ignoring his arrow and sauntering over to the low chain link fence. That athlete's grace, that surety of movement announced him as what he was, just as much as his dark green skin and tusks did. This was an orc warrior. But he wasn't in the orc lands and he didn't need to go and hunt painted cats on the plains. Instead, he was here. He leant the bow up against the fence and then crossed his arms, biceps bulging as he looked down at us. "What can I do for you pretties?"

That seemed to be a call to arms, the orc boys all getting to their feet and strolling over to join their brother, and both Hannah and I took a little step backwards. There was a small fence between us, but it felt like it was little more than a barrier made of wet cardboard.

"Jesus, they're so fucking big…" Hannah hissed, and that just made them all smile.

"Baby, you got no idea," one of them said, his hand sliding south to where his loose-fitting jeans hung on his hips. "You think you won't be able to take it, but trust me, you will. Some practice, and we'll slide right in, one after the—"

"This is how you honour the Mothers?" I asked in a low, deadly tone, and sure enough, each one went perfectly still. "Talking this bullshit out the front of your house? Who do you belong to? Where is your mother?"

"Hey, now, don't be like that," the first one said, putting up his hands.

"We were just mucking around. Don't start going overboard, yeah?"

Hannah turned and looked at me with an incredulous look, but I just stared the 'boys' down. They didn't have the warrior plaits or the short ruffle of my mates. No, these guys had modern haircuts, spiky fauxhawks, and those bloody awful mullets that were making a comeback, but scratch the surface and you got orcs.

"We were sent down here to meet Mama Rosa," I said.

"Right, so come through," the archer said, swinging the gate open and ushering us in. We did so, walking with the cluster of young orcs right the way up to the doorway.

"Mama?" the archer called. "You got visitors!"

Chapter 23

Noises inside the house let us know his call had been heard, and then a larger woman dressed in a brightly coloured muumuu dress appeared in the doorway.

"Yes?"

"Hi, I'm Hannah from Paranormal Control," my friend said, and the woman's eyes narrowed. "And this is my friend, Laila. She stumbled through a portal to Lunor, and we were wondering if you had time to chat?"

"Lunor..." She opened the screen door abruptly. "You better come in."

We filed inside. The house seemed nice, with photos, so many photos, covering the hallway walls. Photos of a much younger Rosa with several hulking orc mates surrounding her. Photos of little boy orcs, the precursors to the dickheads hanging out the front. Photos of the family playing under the sprinklers in the backyard. Photos of them sitting around a massive Christmas feast. It felt insanely invasive to be looking at them and yet...I needed it. This was a life I saw before me—a happy, sprawling, complex, family life, just like any other in Australia.

Orc-ward Encounters

"Turn that bloody music down!" she shouted out the door to her sons. "And get on with tidying up the garden. You know you have work to do!" She then turned to us. "I'm Mama Rosa, but you can just call me Rosa. Come out the back. It's quieter there."

We walked through the house, then out the backdoor to an expansive patio. There was a big outdoor setting there and already seated around it was a group of women.

"Oh, I didn't mean to intrude on a party," I said, stopping where I was.

"Party?" Rosa grinned at that. "Nah, this is just some of the ladies who've come round for a coffee and a chinwag. Girls, this is Hannah and Laila. Laila's just come back from Lunor."

"Has she indeed?" A very elegant Asian woman looked up from her cards, a perfectly shaped eyebrow rising. "And she managed to come back unmated? How is that possible?"

"Um…not quite," I said, taking a seat when it was offered to me. "Three orcs came back with me accidentally and—"

"You're going through first courting," another woman said. She looked human, flopping back in her chair with a grin. "Ahh, I remember that. How the hell are you here, girl? You should be flat on your back the whole time!"

The women all cackled at that.

"This is my friend, Mavis," Rosa said of the other human woman. "She found her band around the same time as I did. Did you fall through that portal at Spencer Street Station? The one in the ladies' toilets? I keep telling Control to do something about that, but…"

"Ah, no. I fell through one in a park outside a nightclub in the city," I said. "I was drunk and—"

"And then you musta got the biggest surprise of your life," another woman said with a broad grin. She was a naga by the look of it, a snake woman with the tail of a snake, but the body of a very beautiful Indian woman. "I'm Siti and this is Lily." She pointed to the Asian woman sitting next to her.

"So how can we help?" Rosa asked, but Mavis had the answers, her smile fading somewhat.

"You're wondering how it works, aren't you?" Her tone was much more gentle, and that unfortunately pricked at me. "How you're going to keep those beautiful men and live a happy life."

"Ah, yeah."

I croaked those words out, not realising that was what was roiling around inside me until someone else said it. I'd felt restless, on edge, but in just a few sentences, Mavis had summed everything up.

"Relationships with paranormals are not easy," Lily said, a long plume of smoke trickling from her nose, even though she wasn't smoking. A second membrane passed over her dark eyes as she regarded me steadily. "You will need to be very sure of what you want. No family holidays to Uluru. No Christmas celebrations on the beach. I can pass as human, so my family can enjoy more freedoms." As she blinked, her eyes turned golden yellow, the pupils becoming long and thin like a snake's.

"But it can be worth it," Rosa said. "You just have to be very sure. That's what first courting is for—to help test that bond. You're attracted to your mates?"

"Of course," I said. "They're amazing."

"But a relationship is more than that. Lunorian orc men are insanely protective and loving, raised to be the perfect husbands, but that means you need to be their perfect wife."

I gulped at that, but Mavis cackled. "Not like a Stepford wife or anything, always having dinner on the table."

"If my husband relied on me to do the cooking, his arse would explode," Siti said with a laconic drawl. "He's such a wuss with chilli!"

"Humans," Lily said with a dismissive snort. "No spice."

"You must be able to give them your whole heart," Rosa continued more seriously. "That's what they need, what they must have if all of you are to be happy. They can't accept anything less."

Silence reigned across the table. Well, as much as it could

here. The boys' music had been turned up again, and I could dimly hear their arguments over it, but as I did so, I found myself imagining. What would it be like if this were my house? If I were sitting around with Hannah and my friends, talking to some girl who was thinking about accepting the suit of her orc mates? If it were my sons in the front yard... I blinked once, twice, then much more rapidly.

"Ohh, that's not going to be a problem," Mavis said with a knowing smile. "You're already there, aren't you, sweetheart?"

I just stared at her, feeling a rush of...what? Of a need to see them, to know where my mates were and what they were doing. To feel their skin under my fingertips, their hair wrapped around my hand and their arms holding me tight. To hear those gruff, rumbly voices, ones that sent a shiver all the way through me. To be snuggled in close, just breathing in their scents.

"It's OK to be worried," Siti said, leaning forward, her fingers toying with a long glass of Coke. "We were all worried at the beginning of our relationships."

"My mother disowned me," Lily said, her expression changing only subtly, but there was real pain there. "*A dragon does not lower herself to mate with a human.*" She shook her head. "My Scott is the most charming human I've ever met. His mother says he could talk the birds out of the trees, and I believe her. He talked me down from my mountain peak when he was back-packing through China, and..."

She shook her head sharply.

"Love is always a gamble. None of us can guarantee an outcome for you, but I will say this. Not trying? Letting it walk past you and out of your life? There's no happiness to be found there, only regret." Lily nodded regally to me. "In some ways, it's the same as a human relationship. All you can do is jump in with two feet and do the best you can."

"Hear, hear!" the others said, raising their glasses, which prompted Rosa to offer us a drink.

. . .

WE STARTED out with just Coke, but as the day went on and each woman shared more stories, tips, and tricks to making a human-paranormal relationship work, the drinks got augmented with a splash of rum, then several splashes of rum, until we were forced to let one of Rosa's sons drive us back to the Centre for Paranormal Control, one of his brothers following behind him in his mum's car.

Apparently, the boys could wear glamours for short periods of time, and Hannah endeared herself, performing the spells for free. Usually, they had to buy little pieces of blessed wood from the 7-11 on the corner to get the same effect. So it seemed as though a burly guy with a deep olive complexion and black hair dropped us off at the centre before handing us the keys and ambling away.

"Thaaaanks, Vuggu!" we called out, waving madly as he went. He turned around, looked at the two of us holding each other up and still managing to sway, and then grinned, shaking his head.

"What the hell happened to you two?" Brenda asked us as we stumbled inside.

"We went to see Mama Rosa," Hannah replied. "She pours very strong drinks."

"Rosa from Monster Street?" Brenda replied with a shake of her head. "You've been drinking orc rum, you idiots."

But we didn't get to dwell on that, as the regular slam of fists on metal dragged our attention elsewhere. I wobbled forward, correcting myself left, then the same again on the right, but I kept moving forward, towards the noise.

"Where is Lay-la?!" someone roared. "Bring us our Lay-la!"

"OMG!" I said, tears pricking my eyes.

"Bestie!" Hannah said, just as emotional. "They fucking love you."

"And are going to tear down that wall to get to you if you don't hustle," Brenda said, putting a hand on each of our shoulders and shoving us forward.

So hustle we did, hearing one last slam of all three of my

mates' fists down on the cage wall before their eyes swung my way.

My mates.

It was true, I knew that now. What had been holding me back was wondering how this shit would work, but I guessed the problem was no one knew exactly how it would work out. If we waited for that, there would be no relationships, but also no new ventures, new ideas, and no new ways of doing things. We would be locked in a cage of what is, always wondering about what might be. I moved closer, thrusting my fingers through the metal grid as my mates clustered closer.

"Lay-la, you were not here when we returned. You have been gone for so long and—" Ghain said.

"And you stink of other orcs," Vargan rumbled, turning me to fucking goo.

"Who touched you, my Lay-la?" Kren demanded. "I will have his head on a spike within the hour, an orc who would dare touch another's mate!"

"No one touched me," I assured him. "I met a few ladies who have orc mates, and we got a bit drunk and their sons helped drive us back."

Their noses worked, dragging in deep breaths, and Ghain turned to Vargan.

"She does stink of honey rum."

"Then she must come inside, so we may bathe the stink of alcohol and other orcs from her skin."

"Oh Jesus, I need to get out of here," Hannah said, then wrapped an arm around me and gave me a squeeze. "I'm gonna sleep this off in one of the fae rooms, but, Laila, remember—no guarantees."

"No guarantees." I nodded, feeling like my head might just pop off as I did so.

Brenda just shook her head and then unlocked the door to let me in, but my mates surged out.

"Jesus fucking Christ," she cursed. "Damn orcs!"

They had me swept up into their arms, their noses buried in my neck and hair, a pair of lips moving in and tasting mine.

"We must clean our mate," one of them rumbled. "And then we must taste her sweetness again. The scent of honey rum makes me hunger."

"OK," I said brightly, laughing as they did just that.

Chapter 24

But when the gate closed with a clang, locking us in, when they shut the door of the bathroom behind us, almost tearing the pants they had been given in their haste to get out of them, all amusement was gone. My clothes were pulled up over my head or down around my ankles, letting me stand only long enough to get free of them before being dragged under the hot water. They were here, my massively tall orc mates.

"Fuck…" I hissed, touching one rock-hard cock, then another. I was a kid in a candy store, and I needed to start licking. Saliva pooled in my mouth as I sucked one cock head, then another, swallowing the super sweet liquid down with ravenous hunger.

"No," Vargan said, pushing me away. "That is for later. We need you now, my Lay-la."

He pushed me against the bathroom wall, and all three of them moved forward, boxing me in.

"An orc cannot let the taste of his intended mate fade in his mouth during first courting," Kren told me.

"Her honey must flavour all things, until it seeps into your very being," Ghain added. "Each one of us must have our taste before we sleep tonight."

"Oh…OK," I replied, it all appearing to make drunken sense. I grabbed a bottle of shower gel, ready to have a quick clean before the tasting began, but this was snatched away by Kren, who then held it up high, drizzling the green liquid all over my breasts.

"Mothers' grace…" Vargan cursed, then put his hand in the soap and began working it oh so sensually all over my body.

Ghain and Kren were quick to help, washing my back, my legs, and even my hair, until I was nothing more than a gooey mess. Then I was sprayed down with the shower head, the pulsating rhythm of the water making my skin come alive right before the shower was shut off. I was bundled up into a towel, then dried off roughly before being dragged into the main bedroom.

"Mm…" Vargan growled. "I admire the strength of these orc males you met today. They made sure you were safe and kept their hands to themselves. I don't know if I could've acted with the same honour if our Lay-la was their intended."

"We would have had to steal her away," Kren agreed.

Ghain shook his head. "But our Lay-la would never undergo first courting with another. The Mothers made her just for us."

And that was what broke me. I stared up at the three of them, concern filling their eyes as tears filled mine. I reached out and stroked Vargan's broad cheeks, Kren's much narrower ones, and Ghain's softer ones, feeling like I needed to map every inch of these beloved faces.

"Yes," I agreed, but they didn't make the link. "Yes, I was made just for you."

"You are?" Vargan asked in wonder, then nodded firmly. "You are. You are our Lay-la, our mate?"

"Yeah, I think I really am."

I was deposited on the bed at that, the three of them covering me with kisses and caresses until I was gasping, but finally, I pulled away. Kren toyed with my nipple, seeming to find inordinate joy in making it pull tighter and tighter until my thighs spread open.

"We must taste you, my mate," Vargan said, his eyes drawn incxorably towards my aching pussy.

"No," I replied. "Well, yeah, sure, but…I need more this time."

"We will fill you with our fingers until you are fit to burst and then stroke that spot inside that makes you spurt," Ghain said, obviously enthusiastic about the idea, but Vargan, he got it. He stared at me as I answered them.

"No, I need more than that," I insisted, more gently now.

"But what more can we…? Oh."

The orcs moved as one, coming to kneel on all sides of me, their hands going to their cocks. I watched in fascination as they swept all the pre-cum off the heads and then pushed their fingers into my mouth, into my cunt, anointing my clit with it until I felt like I was on fire.

"More…" I panted, my insides feeling like they were clenching down hard, but on what? "I need more."

"We are going to cover you with our cum, our mate," Vargan promised. "This will help your body accept us."

"Hmm…" I purred at that idea, reaching up and taking over wherever I could, stroking all those hard cocks, switching from one to the other and then back again as they filled the room with the musical sounds of their groans.

"Mothers' grace!" Ghain yelped as he came first, spraying shot after shot of red hot cum across my tits, my body arching in response. It felt like a million hands and mouths teased, touched, and sucked on my skin, all at once, but as the sensation rose in me, it found nowhere to go. I was just left there, writhing as he reached down, smearing his fluids all over my breasts, paying particular attention to working it into my nipples until they sang with sensation.

"You must swallow this down to take us," Kren rumbled, moving closer. I didn't answer, my lips finding the head of his cock on automatic and sucking on the swollen head, and I only had to bob my head a few times before I got what I needed. I did exactly as he said, swallowing greedily everything he gave me to the increasingly desperate sounds of my mate. I licked the last pulse of his cock head when Kren pulled back slightly, his thick thumb swiping up the cum that had dripped free and pushing it between my lips.

Both Kren and Ghain swept their hands across my whole body as Vargan went to work, stroking his cock in harder, faster strokes, the whole thing going an incredibly angry dark green colour, right as his thighs spread wide. He was angling his hips down between mine, and I gasped out my words of encouragement as his cock got closer, but when the first blast hit, I was fucking lost.

My head was thrown back as pleasure sprayed across me right as his cum did, waking up nerve endings that had never been activated before and tantalising the ones that had. I felt so swollen, bloated with pleasure and need, but right as I tried to adjust to that, their hands came. Vargan had coated my whole cunt with his cum, and now they went to work with it, pushing it inside me, making me ache for more. Hands rubbed it into my clit until I felt like it doubled in size, then sliding their fingers through my folds, making them sensitive beyond belief. Then they pulled away, just kneeling there, staring down at me as I shifted restlessly on the bed.

"I need—"

"We know," Kren said.

"I need more." A deep furrow formed on my forehead.

"We will give you everything we have," Ghain replied, reaching down to stroke his still rigid dick.

"You're still hard?"

"We will be until this is done and you are ours," Vargan explained in a rich, deep voice, one that felt like it stroked me just as thoroughly as their hands. "Because this is the end of first courting."

"No…" I whined, reaching out for them and trying to drag them down, but they remained impervious.

"Yes," he replied. "Because at the end of first courting, comes first mating. We will rise and keep rising until you have all that you need. Our cum will soak into your body and make the changes needed so you can take us without pain. Take all of us."

I stilled at that, looking around me at the circle of hard cocks waiting for me, then reached out with a finger, brushing it across the crown of Vargan's to collect the pearls of pre-cum before pushing it into my mouth.

"Well then, we better get started."

VARGAN'S EXPRESSION shifted from cocky bastard to something much more vulnerable as he moved forward, lowering his body onto mine. He kept his weight on his elbows and stared down at me.

"You've never done this before, have you?" I asked, having a sudden realisation.

"There was no one before you, Lay-la, and there will be none after. If you accept me inside you, into your body, into your heart, I will be your mate forever. The strength of my body will be yours. The fruit of my labour will be yours. The…" He paused, something so terribly vulnerable crossing his face as he tilted his head to fit it into my outstretched hand, closing his eyes, and that seemed to make it easier for him to say. "My whole heart will be as it is—all yours."

"Well, that's good," I croaked out, laughing even as my eyes filled with tears. "Because you've got mine. Just need to seal the deal, big guy."

He nodded at that, moving slowly but surely as the head of his cock notched against me, as he pushed the head in, making me gasp at the sudden intrusion, as he thrust in slow, rocking motions. At first, there was just this glorious feeling of stretching, the heavy swollen pleasure inside me rousing at this extra stimulus, sending long, languorous prickles up and down my spine. Then he kept on coming, feeding more and more of that massive cock into me until I started to get a little scared.

"Shh, shh…" he murmured. "You are our mate. Your body is made to take ours. All other men before us were not worthy and will never get to touch you again. You can take me, I know you can."

And I did, slowly but surely, my nails clawing at Vargan's back as I fought to do so, until finally, he stopped.

"Oh god, oh god…" I kept panting, over and over.

"Forget your puny god," Kren said with a dark smile, leaning down to brush my hair back off my face. "You are the Mothers' daughter now, and they would never steer you wrong."

Lemme tell you, if you ever have a chance to mate with an orc, take it, because the Mothers? They knew their shit. My eyes popped wide as Vargan pulled back, then slammed deep again, each pull-out making my whole body tingle, only for an explosion of pleasure to result as he thrust back in. My hips moved under him, seeking, searching for more of this delirious pleasure, and Vargan chuckled at my enthusiastic response.

"You see, my Lay-la. This is how it was meant to be, how it will always be. You were made to be the mate of orcs, because no one will ever give you what you need like we do."

I responded with a little growl, somehow managing to flip him onto his back, drawing a low chuckle from my mate, right up until I began to move.

"Mothers…" he hissed as I worked myself up and down his massive cock, needing more somehow, ever more. I moved quicker, harder, faster, sure I was obliterating my cervix with all this jackhammer fucking, but somehow, this wasn't all I needed. Vargan's claws pricked my hips, because he couldn't stay still, rutting up into me with shorter, more desperate strokes.

"Vargan…?"

My eyes flicked open, my mouth gasping, my skin screaming for something I couldn't articulate.

"Yes, my love." His thumb pressed against my clit, stroking it with rapid little flicks. "Give me your pleasure, my mate. Take all of me."

I was riding the wave of something which had taken me over,

and it knew what to do. The hard swollen lump at the base of his cock which stopped me from going too far, it was suddenly not such an insurmountable barrier between us. The harder I worked my hips, the deeper it got, opening me, breaking me into pieces, only to be remade again.

"Oh fuck, I'm gonna come!" I yelped, and that was when he took over. He gripped my hips, forcing me down as he thrust up and then there was the most indescribable pressure before *pop!* He was in, all the way in, a throbbing hot presence I felt for a second before the world went sideways.

"Oh fuck! Oh fuck!"

A couple of little pants, and my nails dug into my mate's chest, leaving perfect little crescents, as his roar drowned out mine.

If you've ever seen how fast something can go up in flames when doused with petrol? Well, that was how I felt right now. A great conflagration of pleasure flared up and swallowed me whole, setting my whole body alight, but not just me. My eyes met Vargan's, and I caught the terrible rictus of bliss an orc's face takes on as he experienced something he never had before.

"Vargan..." I panted, my hips jerking with the intensity of what burned between us. "I love you."

He grabbed me then, still pumping his thick seed inside as he rolled me onto my back, burying me in the mattress, covering me with his body, then his kisses.

"I will love you until the Mothers fall from the sky and then beyond that, my Lay-la."

AFTER THINGS SETTLED DOWN, I found out exactly how these knots worked. Vargan and I were locked together for the next twenty minutes or so. Much later, I found out that was why bands formed. An orc was awfully vulnerable when locked down tight inside a woman, so his band kept guard as he took his fill and then passed their mate onto the next orc to satisfy.

I found I was not at all concerned about being knotted by

Vargan. I nestled down into his chest, snuggling into that hard wall as he stroked my back, as he said my name again and again. Little kisses, little touches, so many I couldn't keep track, because this was us now. We were mated, tied tighter than any human couple, and we wouldn't ever be separated again. Finally, he was able to pull free, dragging an uncomfortable moan from me at the feeling of emptiness.

"You ache for more, my mate?" Kren asked, kissing the answer from my lips. I reached up and pulled him on top of me, glorying in that massive muscular weight. "I have all that you need and more."

My fingers dug into his hips and hauled him forward, both of us groaning as he sank inside me.

"Definitely more."

Chapter 25

Kren seemed determined to take things much slower, which did my fucking head in. He smiled down at me as he laid me on the bed, dipping down to kiss me but pulling away as soon as I reached for him.

"Kren..."

"I know," he said with a gentle smile. "I know, my mate. I can feel your need here" —he patted his chest— "and I can feel it here."

His hand swivelled up and down his cock, and I followed his every move, reaching up to help, but my hands were pushed away.

"Not this time, my mate, my love." A sigh escaped me at that word, another as he leaned over, kissing me gently. "I have waited for so long to find you." A tiny frown formed and then faded away. "I have dreamed of you so many times, always just out of reach." Another kiss, a slow one this time. "Let me have this, have you, and later, you can have me."

OK, I was down with this plan, particularly as he moved over me, the massive contrast between his body and mine making me feel deliciously vulnerable. Kren could break me in two with little effort, but instead, he put me back together. His teeth nipped at my neck, kissing me, marking me, making me arch up under him as his lips dropped lower. He groaned as he got to my breasts, kissing one nipple, then another, before settling between my legs.

"Yes..." I hissed as I felt his thick length brush against me, an answering ache winding tighter inside me. "Kren, I need—"

"I know, my love." He reared up and took my hands, placing them firmly above my head. "Keep your naughty hands where they are and let me work. When we come together, the Mothers themselves will stop to watch."

"Now, please, Kren."

"Kren, you make our mate beg!" Ghain hissed.

"Because prolonging the pleasure makes it greater," Kren replied, shooting him a hard look. "Because I want our mate to have every pleasure I can wring from her body. Because I want her screams to rouse the wolf people next door and make them howl with frustration that they are not similarly blessed with such an incredible mate."

Well, OK then.

Kren's hands went to my breasts, covering them almost entirely with his massive hands, a faraway look in his eyes as he teased my nipples to life. He seemed to drop down into some space I couldn't understand but got all the benefit from. Slick oozed out of me, the aching emptiness within growing, while my body shifted and twisted on the bed as he built something inside me, but I bore it for him. If he wanted to give me this gift, I had to trust him, and I realised I did.

My eyes flicked open, and he nodded, a strange soft smile on his face.

"Now you understand."

And with that came the rewards. He fell down upon me like a wolf on its prey, sucking, scoring his teeth across my skin, licking, and then moving his cock until the head rested on my clit and the length was nestled between my folds. There was no way for him to push inside me at this angle, something that had my hands clawing at the blankets, but then he began to rock.

Like a massive thick finger, it rubbed at my clit, at my cunt, my entrance aching to be filled, but still, he moved. My cries got louder, my own hips moving now, trying to change his angle so he would push inside me, but I couldn't. He chuckled cruelly, his hips pressing mine down hard against the bed, the increased pressure sending fireworks of sensation through me, but always ones that made me want more and never get it.

"Kren…" I gasped out his name as his pace grew faster, the need to wrap my arms around him building, but I kept my position.

"Kren!" He shifted the angle, his cock working the hood of my clit back and forth, back and forth, my cries becoming ragged. He watched me the whole time with perfect focus, seeming to read every response and reaction, searching for something.

"Oh god, Kren, I can't…"

I was babbling now, my body screaming with need. My cunt kept clenching down, reminding me of what I was lacking, of how hollow I felt.

"I'm empty," I finally sobbed. "So empty. Kren, I need—"

"I will always give you what you need," he told me, moving us quickly, expertly, so that he was on his knees and one of my ankles was resting on his chest. He kissed the bone there, and then I chanted yes over and over as he lined himself up and then drove into me.

The shock of having so much cock right after I'd had none had my eyes flicking open. A long, strangled sound escaped me as I felt it, every damn inch working inside me.

"So tight…" he rasped out. "So good, my Lay-la. Mothers' grace, so good!"

Whatever ironclad control he'd been using, that began to fray. Those big strong hands gripped me now as hard as they dared, holding me fast as he rutted inside me in fast brutal strokes. Vargan's efforts, they made it so much easier now, my body opening up like a flower, welcoming Kren in deeper and deeper until he threw himself down over me. He hung there, and we teetered together on some kind of precipice until he let out a godawful bellow and pushed his knot in.

I had a lifetime of knotted sex to look forward to, and I thanked God or the Mothers for just that. It was like orcs had been created for women, as the huge lump made missing the G-spot an impossibility. Instead, with every stroke, much slower now, he pushed down hard, resulting in a deep, dark kind of pleasure.

"Kren. Oh, Kren…" He just stared, watching everything, completely in the moment, and I wrapped my arms around his neck and kissed him for that.

Things got more frantic, messier now, our bodies rocking together over and over, finding a pace we both could match. This was what being a mate was about—working together for the betterment of our band, each giving to the other everything we had to give. I stared into those dark eyes and knew then that had been his plan all along.

"I need you to come, my mate," he said in a gentle tone. "Come on my cock so I can give you everything I have."

And just like that, I did.

My whole body tensed as I clung to him, my torso and hips rolling in waves that he just surfed through. I came and I came and I came, gripping his cock, his knot, trying to pull him down with me into this endless spiral of pleasure.

"Lay-la!"

I went limp as I felt his hips slam against mine and stay there, cum jetting over and over inside me. Then there were kisses, messy kisses and gasped declarations, but the one that stuck in my mind was this.

"You are the Mothers' grace, my mate. You are her beauty and her strength. You are everything to me." And then Kren held me close, smothering any response from me as I listened to his heart racket in his chest.

"I love you," I said in a small, muffled voice, which forced him to jerk back, looking down at where I was nestled into his chest.

"Truly?"

"Of course," I replied sleepily. "I'll always love you. You are my mate."

"Always," he agreed, kissing me much more softly now. "And I love you, my mate."

GHAIN WAS the one that stirred things up again, stroking my back and my hair as we waited for Kren's knot to go down, but those long, catlike strokes just had me rousing again. I'd never felt anything like this, usually happy if I came once, but not now. His sure fingers made me shiver, something that made the other two orcs chuckle.

"You make her clench down hard on my shaft," Kren complained, but there was pleasure there too, evident in his sensual tone. "She's milking me dry."

"One of my fathers told me as much when I became an adult," Ghain said, sliding a possessive hand down my front. "He said if you keep stimulating your mate, she will expel the other orc's lock more quickly." As if on cue, I felt Kren slide free, a rush of cum spilling across my thighs. "And then be ready for more."

"Mm…" I agreed, nodding blindly. "Definitely more."

"It shortens things," Vargan grumped.

"It makes more than once possible in a night," Ghain countered, pulling me from Kren's arms and into his. I was held against his chest, looking down wearily at the others, who were still hard. His hand strayed across my inner thigh, then swept up, tickling my folds with just the tips of his fingers. "It means we can fill our mate over and over with the seed that she needs."

The low, dirty growl that came from the three of them, that was what set me alight again. They obviously had wild ideas about a sex marathon, but I wasn't so sure. My body felt heavy and tired.

But not too tired. Ghain's caresses became more insistent, relighting the fire inside me, my other mates laughing as my thighs spread wider, my hips arching up into his hand. One more, definitely one more.

"And more again, my mate," Ghain said, pushing me down onto the bed, his fingers never losing contact with my clit. "You need everything we have to give you and then just a little bit more."

I went to contradict that, but he pushed two thick fingers into me, and apparently, that was all I needed to convince me.

"More," I agreed with a frantic nod. "Yes, Ghain, more."

Chapter 26

"I need to open you up more, my mate," Ghain told me, and it was evident why. His cock wasn't the longest, but it was definitely the thickest. "I need you to take me, all of me."

"Mm..." I purred, moving to do just that. His cock was like that all night Netflix binge when you have work the next day—you knew you probably shouldn't, but you couldn't help but reach for that remote and throw on another episode. I was pushed down onto the bed firmly, a hand pinning me there as he nipped off several of his talons, then licked his fingers slowly. I found myself transfixed by the sight, my body already tightening in anticipation.

"I have wanted this for so long, breathing in your sweet scent, feeling your body against mine. I need you so much, my mate."

His vulnerable tone had me pausing for a moment, staring up at him.

"Ghain?"

"I lost my way and didn't trust in the Mothers' grace. I feared we would never find our mate, our territory being so far from the human settlements. My heart cried out for the one who would complete us, over and over, until I became numb to its call. Then we found you."

I wanted, needed to reply, but he pushed his fingers inside me at that point, making my body tense at the sudden intrusion.

"Shh, shh," he said, rubbing a soothing hand over my stomach. "You are made to take this, to take me."

And so he moved slowly, corkscrewing his fingers in, feeling my body relent and accept him, before pulling back and then thrusting his hand in and out until his fingers moved freely. His hand was pulled away to the sound of my cries, then he thrust his fingers back in again, adding another.

It was a stretch, would be a stretch, I realised, but there was a pleasure to be found from that. It made me aware of my body in ways I'd never felt before the orcs. Ghain watched me respond with almost a shy regard, but once his eyes locked with mine, they couldn't look away. He watched my lips fall open, listened to my pants as he forced his fingers deeper, then smiled as he curled them up.

"Fuck…"

"She likes that," Vargan said, collapsing down on the bed beside me. "That spot, it always makes her so wet."

"And open," Ghain said on a groan. "I can feel her parting around my fingers."

"Wait until she's taken your knot," Kren said, moving behind me to rest my head in his lap. "My fathers tried to warn me of such things, but…" He traced a slow finger through my hair, smiling down at me as I slowly came apart. "The experience is incomparable, Ghain. You will never know a moment's pleasure that matches it."

"But you must open our mate well or you will hurt her," Vargan instructed, lifting my knees up to my chest.

Straight away, Ghain's fingers slid deeper, all three of them making approving noises like I'd achieved some great feat or something, but then I realised what else came with this. Ghain wasn't just helping dilate me enough to take his thick cock without pain. They were opening me up emotionally as well as physically. I could feel it in the way the other two stroked me, coaxed me, and praised me through the process. As they kissed away my gasps and made sure I had more. As they worked together to stroke me, tease me, spoil me.

What a funny idea that was, that I could be ruined by pleasure. They seemed to have no such qualms, winding me tighter and tighter, until finally, Ghain lent down, staring into my eyes before kissing my mouth.

"You're ready to be mine now."

"Yes..." I nodded enthusiastically as he reached for me and hauled me up onto his knees, and for a second, there was just him and me, facing each other. He shivered when I ran my finger up his cock but was able to tolerate it as long as I didn't do anything else. Then he moved closer, casting a warm shadow over me. His hand reached up, stroking my cheek with the back of his knuckles.

"I need you to ride me, my mate, to take me deep inside you." I bit my lip as I felt that inside me, how it would go. "You'll be able to control it, how fast, and then you'll take your pleasure like a queen." He moved in closer, his unruly hair falling over one eye, but that didn't stop him from staring into mine. "We can do this. We will be joined, become mates in body as well as heart."

His hand settled over my chest, and I reached up and placed mine over his, feeling the slow thud of his heartbeat. Then he nodded, taking my hands in his as he sat down on the bed, pulling me onto top of him to straddle his hips.

There was something magical about mating with each and every one of them, but right now? Ghain was the final one of my mates I would take, and then we would be a band in earnest. His eyes burned into mine as I reached down, grabbing his cock by the root, his brows knotting as I gripped his base, and then I moved my body until my wetness brushed over his swollen crown.

"Mothers..." Ghain hissed.

"Such a velvety feeling, brother," Vargan said with lazy amusement.

"I feared I would be unmanned the moment I pushed inside her," Kren added, because apparently, we were doing the director's cut version of mating, complete with commentary, but Ghain didn't pay any attention to them. It was all about me, everything, and it always would be with these guys. That was what I'd learned when I was at Mama Rosa's.

"Women think that they want orc mates, once they get past the tusks and the green skin," she said, staring off into the distance. "They think they want a man or men who are devoted entirely to them, and I will admit it's a beautiful thing."

"Mm hmm," Mavis affirmed.

"But I'll tell you what I will tell any woman my sons seek to take as a mate. It's a tremendous responsibility as well. They will do literally anything for you." I thought of tragic Mahk and his administering of Susie's medicine. *"It's in their nature, it's in the way they are raised. My boys have gotten wild, listening to and watching human TV shows and movies, wanting to be warriors in a world that doesn't need them, but when they find their mates, they'll be the same."*

Her dark eyes flicked to meet mine.

"If you want everything from an orc mate, you have to give back everything you have. It's the only way. Not ignoring healthy boundaries or anything, but if there's a corner of your heart unclaimed, they'll want it and need it. Otherwise, you're not mated. You're cohabiting, sleeping together, whatever you want it to be, but you're not truly connected, and they'll know. Every day, they'll get up, go about their day, needing something they aren't going to get. So be sure, young Laila. Be very sure."

I felt it right then, as I lowered myself down, Ghain's hands cupping my butt. There was something so much more intimate about this, his eyes staring into mine the whole time.

"I love you," I said, and they echoed that, Kren and Vargan clustering close, energy rising along with arousal. I pushed my fingers into Ghain's hair, shoving it back off his hard warrior's face, tracing my finger along his tusk as I sank deeper.

Orc-ward Encounters

He was big, so fucking big in all ways, I felt uniquely helpless, held like a doll in his arms, so small in comparison to his muscular bulk, struggling to take him in deeper and deeper thrusts, my body feeling like it was being pierced through, but in a way I fucking craved. I made frustrated little growls as I struggled to get him fully inside me, everyone encouraging and praising my efforts, but it was so fucking worth it. Fingers teased at my clit, making this relentless intrusion into something magical.

"Lay-la…my mate…"

I was strung out, but Ghain was right there with me, our bodies fighting, fighting, until finally, we both lost and were forced to just surrender.

"Oh fuck…"

I collapsed down onto his chest, and he held me close, so tight, so that when we moved, it was together, thrusting, thrusting, trying to physically approximate that rushing sensation of them as they broke everything inside me down and then remade me anew.

It got so messy after that. What my body was doing was almost irrelevant as I felt Ghain, felt all of them so deep in my heart, tears streamed down my face. Vargan and Kren voiced concerns, but Ghain knew. He took my face in his hands, sucking down my cries of pleasure, of pain, of need, of everything we were. Then, right as my heart felt like it was going to burst, his knot pushed in.

I panted frantically, sucking on his lips and tongue, right before it came.

This was more than just coming, I knew that as soon as I felt an incredible sense of lightness fill me. It was like I was dipped in gold or turned from flesh to sunbeams or some other nonsensical thing. I dunno, it just was. We weren't in bed in some shed out on the outskirts of Melbourne. For the first time, I felt what they kept talking about, the Mothers' grace, because I had no other words for it. As Ghain's cum jetted inside me, as Vargan and Kren's splattered across my skin, we were all filled with a light, a pleasure that had to have come from a divine source, because it overtook the four of us.

"I love you," I said to Ghain, to all of them, and I felt his lips against my neck, his mighty muscles holding me tight.

"There is nothing in my heart beyond you, my Lay-la. Nothing. You are the moons and the stars and…"

Ghain's words failed because there was no need now. Rosa, Mavis, they hadn't told me about this because they couldn't. I can't really describe it for you now. Some things, they're beyond description, so intense, so immense, that words just fail and fade in response.

LATER, much later, we came back to ourselves. We could feel the bed now, the clasp of each other's bodies, hear the regular rasp of our breath. Ours, that was what I felt the hardest, my individual senses returning but another coming with us.

"This is why we can't work apart, our mate," Vargan said quietly, knowing now that I felt it. "However we find our way in this world, it must be together."

I nodded, understanding perfectly for the first time.

Chapter 27

I quit my job. I hadn't wanted to, and my employer, my colleagues were shocked by my surprise resignation, but after taking the three orcs as mates, something burned inside me. It was a fire we shared, one that flared to life when we looked at each other, first in our den, then in the big cafeteria, once the orcs had proven they could co-exist with other species without violence.

My orcs were actually surprisingly peaceful, as long as no one came too close to me nor appeared to want to hurt me. I didn't think anyone would, but the message was sent pretty clearly by the orcs' body language, and not just that. They went to class every day and were apparently diligent students, devouring knowledge about our world, their world now, but when they returned from class? I was taken over and over, teased and suckled and marked with their seed, until whatever need inside them turned down lower.

But all of this was a holding pattern, a beautiful, sensual holding pattern that I was tempted to just lose myself in but couldn't. They had provided for me, found me food, clothing, water in Lunor, and now I needed to do the same. So one day, after prolonged kisses and hugs goodbye, I'd slipped out with Hannah and gone back to Monster Street.

IT WASN'T REALLY A STREET, I learned, but a suburb of sorts, and we were on the outskirts of it, standing in front of a big red brick home with a huge allotment of land behind it. The blocks here were freaking massive, with a long stretch of grass and bush attached. It was that which sold me on the place before we even got inside. I felt like such a bitch, taking the orcs from their territory, but maybe this would go some way to alleviating things for them?

"Ladies!" Manoli, the guy with the statuary place we'd met on the main street, had turned up in his car with his brother-in-law, the landlord, in tow. "You've decided to settle on the street?"

"Yeah." We were introduced to his brother-in-law, Theo, who looked Hannah and me over with an evaluative eye. "This place looks amazing."

"It's even better inside," Manoli enthused, walking up to the front door.

"So this will be a Centre lease contract for a year under the usual terms?" Theo asked Hannah.

"I've got pre-approval and everything," she said, handing him a sheaf of papers. He flicked through them before nodding and giving them back.

"Well, let's take a look at the house then."

The thawing of Theo's cool demeanour came from the fact the Centre for Paranormal Control paid your rent for the first year. Landlords liked that security and apparently could charge a fairly generous rent. Manoli unlocked the front door, extolling the different virtues of the place, but I didn't hear that much of it. I just saw the blank walls, the clean floors, and then a whole lot of something else juxtaposed on top of it.

Just like Rosa's place, our walls would be covered with photos and mementos. Memories caught forever, frozen and displayed in their frames. Our children would clamber up and down the long halls, would sleep in their beds in one of the four bedrooms. The master bedroom was massive, big enough to install one of the mega beds we enjoyed in the werewolf den we'd been sleeping in, and we would wake up every morning here, together. Because unlike the dire message my endocrinologist had given me before, the doctor at the Centre had quite a different message.

"I don't think you'll have any problems conceiving when you're ready, Laila. I know what you've been told, but your androgen levels as well as oestrogen and progesterone are all within normal ranges. Have you been having the same problems with facial hair?"

My hand strayed to my chin, and I realised I hadn't plucked anything out for ages. As my fingers passed over my skin, I didn't feel any of the same prickle of thick hairs.

"No, I haven't."

Dr Angie nodded and smiled.

"Sometimes, that's what happens. We have humans and paranormals come together, and it helps or it hinders. Whatever is going on with you since you took the orcs as mates, it's agreeing with you. When or if you are ready to start trying for a baby, come and see me and I'll take the implant out."

"So what do you think, Laila?" Hannah asked me as I stood in the kitchen, staring blankly at the very nice set-up.

"I think we'll take it."

THEN MOVING DAY CAME.

"So can we open our eyes now, my mate?" Vargan asked in an ever so cranky voice. "We are out in the open, and there may be dangers we need to attend to."

I was leading the three of them into the house with their eyes closed. I held Ghain's hand, who held Kren's, who held Vargan's, and we made a slow, stumbling chain of people walking up the new driveway.

"There are no dangers," I assured him.

"You do not know this for sure," Kren said. "That painted cat—"

"Painted cats or their equivalents are only found overseas or in zoos," I said. "Just a few more steps."

"It is clean here," Ghain said with approval, sniffing blindly. "The air smells fresh. There are trees and—"

"And open your eyes and check it out for yourself," I said.

They all looked around them wildly, but I just waved to Bruce and Hannah, who were waiting on the verge, leaning against the truck that had brought us over here. We would be using it to move all my junk into the house, and theirs.

It turned out the Centre had kept our portal open. Not forever, but they just wanted an easy way to get back to Lunor if we changed our minds. We hadn't, but we did want to go back for one last thing.

To say goodbye.

It concerned me. My mates had friends and family too, and I wondered if we could bring Judith through and situate her on Monster Street, but they seemed to think that wouldn't work.

"My mother must stay near the bones of my fathers," Vargan had said. "Our cave was theirs, before it was mine. Without the memory of them, she would waste away."

So we walked inside the front door of our new house, and I nervously watched them check it out.

"It is big, much bigger than the den at the Centre," Kren said approvingly, opening his arms wide, as if that was a measure of worth.

"And it has many rooms." Vargan turned to me with a heated look. "We must work hard to fill them, my mate."

"Soon," I promised.

I'd explained about contraception and the idea that women waited until they felt ready to have children. It'd been a strange idea to them, but their strong grounding in feminine choice made it something they could readily accept. Rather than talking endlessly about having babies, they talked often about the ways women came to feel ready, their devious minds seeking a way to try and accelerate that process.

"But look at this…"

Orc-ward Encounters

Ghain's voice, it had us all turning, following him into the kitchen, staring out the big window above the sink, which gave you a panoramic view of the block behind. Our block, for now. The backdoor was open, and we all filed through, but while I stood on the back step, they went so much farther. Ghain let out an almighty whoop, throwing open his arms and spinning around, Kren running past him, towards the tree line, scaling one with startling ease before dropping back to the ground.

"You chose well, my mate." Vargan came behind me, putting an arm around my shoulders and then pulling me in close. "We had fields to run in at the Centre, but this, this is a territory. Orcs need a territory to defend."

I thought of what was about to come next, turning around to face him and feeling a little worry rise.

"We can go back," I said for the umpteenth time. "We are going back."

"What?"

I hadn't told him this yet. Well, not that we were doing this today, as soon as they guys were finished whooping it up.

"We're going through the portal, one last time, to grab anything you might need or want, because…"

"Because they are going to close it forever," Vargan said with a slow nod. "We have chosen and we chose you. There are things we wish to retrieve. Gifts for your parents are among them."

It galled them that I hadn't introduced them to my parents. It was on the cards and I had a plan, but there were some elements I had to wait for first.

"OK, well, let's round up the troops, because we're going through today."

"Today? But we need—"

"Your axes? Got them, big guy. They were returned to you all after moving out of the Centre. You've passed all your classes with flying colours, and people there feel comfortable that you'll only use them in dire need. I'm pretty sure Brenda put in a good word for you too."

A look passed over Vargan's face then, one I didn't quite understand. Relief was in there, so was pride, but there was also satisfaction and…a whole bunch of other stuff that was purely orc. He took my hand in his and then shouted to the others.

"Enough playing! We return to the land of the Mothers one last time, my brothers. We must go!"

The other two jerked to attention and then came running towards us.

"We return to Lunor? But we decided to stay," Kren said.

"We go one last time to retrieve anything we need from our old cave and bring it to our new one," Vargan informed them. They all nodded, and then we filed out through the house.

IT WAS late in the day, so by the time we got back to the city, to our portal, night was falling. It was a Monday, so the clubs weren't open and there were few people around. Hannah squeezed my hand as we walked over, all of us dressed now in what looked like workman's coveralls to legitimise our presence. And they all wore glamours.

"God, it's been so long since I've worn one of these, working on your case," Hannah said, reaching behind her to scratch at her shoulder blades. "I forgot how bloody uncomfortable a glamour can be."

"I feel like a heavy weight is pushing down on me," Ghain said, touching his face. Well, not his face. He was still super tall with dark hair and eyes, but now his skin was a deep olive, his mouth just like mine, and somehow, that hurt to look at.

"And my tusks, they still feel like they're here," Kren said.

"They look like they aren't to humans, that is all. Do you not remember the class we attended on glamours?" Vargan rumbled.

"It's OK." I put a hand on Vargan's arm, then all of my mates. "You're all feeling uncomfortable."

"Very uncomfortable," Kren grumbled, moving his face, making grotesque expressions as he tested the way the glamour made it feel.

Orc-ward Encounters

"You're pretending to be something you're not," I said to Hannah, who stopped scratching and then just looked at me, then nodded, a small smile forming.

"And this all feels seriously awkward." I took a long breath and let it out. "Looks like we've come full circle now."

Bruce snorted and then unlocked the temporary barrier around the portal. He stepped back and then ushered us in.

When the sounds of drums came, the orcs jerked their heads, but I just shook mine, forging on, pausing only to look up at the moon above us, full of course, full of the Mother's power, even if she was weaker in this world. Then I moved, finding the place in between unerringly and stepping through into Lunor.

Chapter 28

I hadn't felt the Mothers' power the last time I came through here, but I felt it now. That curious lightness, a beauty, a radiance that seemed to burn forever inside me, I gasped as I felt it flare harder here.

"Mothers' grace…" Kren said in a low, reverential tone, the others saying the same.

"We truly know now, what that means," Vargan said with a nod. "Now we must follow that grace to its natural conclusion."

It had just got dark here, so we picked our way easily through the trees, walking in the curious quiet of the forest, the only sounds coming from my clumsy steps and the birds that woke at night.

Unlike last time, there were no barriers, no Urzog to try and stop us. There would be no barriers, I realised, because we walked in the Mothers' light. I tried to remember this, store this memory away so I could pull it out later. I wanted my sons to know this, to feel this as best as we could achieve in our one-mooned world. This was their birthright, and that made the trek back to the cave a somewhat sombre one.

We walked up to Judith's cabin first, and she appeared at the railing with a gentle smile on her face.

"You know, Mother?" Vargan asked.

"Of course. You will too, when your sons' time comes. The Mothers' light, it is a generous thing, flaring brighter and brighter with each connection."

"And you have been well?" Ghain asked, anxiously scanning her and her dwelling. "We have been gone for some time."

"You left for Mahk's this morning," she replied with a gentle smile. "Such is the way of magics, I assume. A capricious thing, but that's not why you have come. You wear the clothes of another's world, and you smell of another place."

"We have found our mate, Mother," Vargan said, holding my hand up, our fingers tightly laced.

"So you have, my darling boy, and where she goes, so must you."

I saw it then, the way it was with mothers and why everyone spoke of their grace in this world. A mother's life, a parent's life, was one of sacrifice. You let your children go, over and over, to school, to friends' and families' places, perhaps to university, and then, into adulthood. The moment you had them, you were constantly having to practise letting them go until you passed.

"Don't be sad, my warrior boy," Judith said, reaching up and brushing away a single tear from the hard planes of Vargan's face as he lent down, then wrapping her arms around his neck as best she could. "I would've been far sadder if you never found your Lay-la. One such as you should never go without finding the other half of his heart. You have my blessing, my son. Go into this other world and know you carry with you the love of the Mothers, of this mother."

They pressed their foreheads together, and for a moment, they just were, a silent moment of communion, but then Judith pulled away and went to Kren.

"I see you, my warrior boy," she said to Kren and he bent his head, just as Vargan had, letting her hug him as well. "You keep my boys safe now. That Ghain and his dreaming and my

Vargan, he lets things get too serious. Protect them from themselves, and they will do the same for you. You have my blessing, son of my heart if not the son of my body."

Again, the same moment of quiet contemplation before she pulled away.

"My sweet warrior boy," she said, throwing her arms wide to Ghain, and he swept in, wrapping his arms around her. "You must keep the heart of the band safe, protect the Mothers' grace that burns inside you all, because it burns the hottest in you." Ghain flushed at that, just a subtle darkening of his skin that you'd only notice if you'd stared at the plains of his face for many hours. "You have my blessing, son of my heart if not the son of my body."

I thought they were done, after Ghain pressed his forehead to hers for some time, then pulled away again. My feet shifted, feeling a restlessness not to get away, but as a means to process the guilt.

"Paranormals like me," Hannah said to me one afternoon as we sat at the outdoor setting at the back of the Centre, *"we walk in two worlds—the one of humans and the one of our own kind."*

The guys were practising their barbequing skills, which would be a massive disappointment to American readers. I'd seen all these Food Network shows where barbequing is this careful, considering culinary art, the choice of fuel and meats carefully paired. That wasn't what my men learned.

"You're going to have to be careful of that," she advised with a sidelong look. *"You see this with humans in Australia, where a part of the population is almost affronted by the fact people come to this country with vibrant cultures of their own. That speaking another language or doing things differently is somehow an attack on the culture people have joined. Your mates, they have their own culture."*

"I know."

"No, Laila, you don't. Not totally. They've probably told you all they could, but it's not the same as growing up in Lunor, of seeing, hearing, noticing unconsciously all the different things that make them Lunorian orcs. It's why Mama Rosa's boys are different to your mates, as your sons will be. They will be a fusing of both your cultures, but that takes work."

"How will I manage that?" I asked, my hand wrapping tighter around the glass of Coke I was nursing.

"Whenever there is a chance for them to be themselves, make sure there's space for that," she replied. "They've decided not to go back to Lunor, so you need to bring as much of Lunor as you can into your home."

I watched them burn the shit out of the meat in the time-honoured tradition of Australian men. We always make sure the beer is OK, but the food? There were no gorgeous saucy spare ribs or smokey brisket. Nah, we had carbon encrusted steak, sausages with long stripes of black down their lengths, still pink in the middle. Then slices of potato that were crunchy but seared black on the outside, along with crispy fried onions. They walked over, congratulating themselves on their efforts, bringing with them the big bottle of tomato sauce that Australians always use to right all of our culinary wrongs.

"We have prepared the food in the manner of your people, yes?" Vargan asked, putting the platter of food before us. "We did it alone, away from the women, and we talked 'shit' as we did it. You have the salads prepared in the small receptacles?"

"I do," I said, putting a plastic bag on the table as Hannah and I worked to set out the coleslaw and potato salad from the local Woolworths. "So when you meet my dad, you should totally follow these rituals, but the rest of the time, you should cook the food the way you would normally."

"Oh thank the Mothers," Ghain said, spitting out his sausage on the grass. "Why do your people ruin perfectly good food this way?"

"Is it the taste of charcoal you like?" Kren asked. "Perhaps we could grind some up and you could add it as a condiment."

"No, no, the orc way is definitely better. Almost any way is better than the traditional Aussie BBQ. Even my people are starting to shift away from cremating our food," I replied. "And there are some spare steaks and sausages I kept aside." I pulled out the last thing in the bag. "So you can cook things properly."

WHY DID it have to be like this? I thought as I watched Judith pull away from Ghain. *Why does someone have to win and someone have to lose?* That wasn't quite what was happening, but as I saw them say their final farewells, it felt like it. Maybe I could find a way to live here? Maybe I could…?

We were right back where we started again, torn between two worlds, but they were willingly letting go of theirs and I needed to honour that sacrifice. My mates turned my way as the flame in my heart burned that bit hotter, tears filling my eyes as I acknowledged what they were doing. Then Judith turned to me.

"My daughter…"

That took me by surprise, as did the warmth in her tone, her hands coming to rest on my shoulders for a moment before she drew me into her embrace. I hugged her back, and despite the fact I'd only met her a day ago in her world, I found a tremendous comfort in this.

"In our world, there is always someone who leaves and someone who stays," she said. "Most times, it's the woman who leaves her world, but that is simply because the humans will not tolerate our orcs within their midst. They like very much the protection from the raiders, but prefer that to happen out of sight. So I know what my boys will go through."

She pulled away, still gripping my shoulders, staring into my eyes.

"You feel the Mothers' grace now?" I nodded. "Keep it burning bright then, my love, because no matter what happens, it is the moons' light in a world of darkness, keeping the monsters at bay."

And then she drew me close, her forehead coming to rest against mine, and that was when I felt it.

My mates would never get this from my parents. It wasn't that they wouldn't want this link with my mates, but we humans were not equipped with such light. That was what came rushing in, hot and immediate, filling me up in ways that surprised me, even after taking her sons as my mates, because she was bequeathing me something.

When she broke away, she stumbled slightly, Vargan swooping in to steady her, but she just waved him away.

"When you have your sons, you give them that light," she

said, some urgency in her voice. "It's how we've always done things here. We pass it from one to the other, and for the most part, that's how it works. You get some like Urzog, who turn their backs on the Mothers' light, but not your sons."

"Of course," I said. "But who's going to look after you?"

"The grand chieftain's wife has been after me for years to come and live with her. We were friends back when we grew up on the plains. She has strings of young sons who can support two old women. I was only waiting here for this—to see my sons mated." Judith gave a definite nod. "So this was always going to be farewell."

She placed her hand on her heart, the orcs doing the same, and then all four of them brought them out so their palms faced the others, then she turned without a word to walk back into her house, no doubt to pack it up.

As we needed to.

"Come, Lay-la." Vargan said, taking my hand and walking us up the path to the cave.

THIS FELT WRONG, but it was a necessary evil, I told myself, as I watched them fetch and carry items important to them. Food items would be donated, for they would send a bird to the grand chieftain so that others could come and take what they wished from this cave. Lots of other things were also left. I saw them pick up and discuss the merits of bringing so many things, then deciding against it. Elf crystals were redundant in a world with electric hot water. A cooking plate wasn't needed when we could buy a BBQ. In the end, they just took their weapons, more for sentimental purposes than anything, loading themselves up in a way that would no doubt alarm Bruce. Then they looked back at the cave and nodded. It was done, but somehow, I felt I wasn't.

"Should we…? Don't we…?"

"This is what we needed to come back for," Vargan said, opening a startlingly big bag and pulling out chunks of gold and raw gemstones. "Presents for your family, for Ha-nah, to use to barter for the goods we need."

And right then, I saw Draco and his hungry eyes as he eyed Frag's box of ores and stones.

"Don't go giving them away for a loaf of bread," I said, closing his hand over the bag. "I know where we need to go to sell them."

"As you say, my mate. And now, we return."

They whistled for their messenger bird to come, had written a note for the grand chieftain, but something made me put my hand on Kren's arm when he went to send it off.

"Maybe we should just let Judith tell the chieftain," I said.

I don't know why, but making that final step, turning this cave over to another band, it just felt wrong. Like I knew it would happen, that Judith would inform the chieftain and the necessary steps would take place, but… I didn't want it to be us that pulled the trigger, and I couldn't understand why.

"If you wish," Kren said, setting the pencil and the message down on the table. Then he gave the bird a handful of seed before sending it back to whichever tree it'd been hanging out in.

I FELT like my feet were heavy, that there was a melancholy hanging over the trip back to the portal, even though there was no evidence of it. I could feel my mates' hearts within mine, the rapid flicker of excitement, of anticipation. We were fulfilling their lifelong dream, setting up house as a band, moving towards what they saw as a glorious future. I felt that too, but when we came to the portal, I looked back, stared at the Mothers in the sky, and wondered at the path they'd put us on.

And for good reason.

The sound of someone blundering through the forests let us know we weren't the only ones here. The orcs had their axes out and they surrounded me in seconds, but there was no enemy here. Well, not ours. Susie came stumbling through the trees, blinking muzzily as she saw us, peering as she got closer.

"There you are!" She held out her arms, like we were old friends or something, but my mates didn't move, not an inch, not even when Mahk came behind her. "So did you find it? That pesky little portal?"

OK, this bitch was stoned again and about to go home, so I guessed there was a symmetry to that.

"We did," I replied, watching Mahk's face, not hers. He was quietly stoic, but I could feel it now, the fire that Susie was so divorced from. His burned so low, starved of fuel for so long, but still, it flickered. "It'll take you to Australia. Melbourne, actually, but I know some people who'll be able to get you home."

"Oh my gahd!" she said, throwing her arms out. "Yes, yes, yes! Well, let's get this damn show on the road. Mama needs a proper damn shower."

It took her a painfully long time to see Mahk, to remember he was even there. Our silence seemed to prompt her, that and our reluctance to act on her orders. Seeking a more malleable assistant, she turned to Mahk instinctively, and that was when I saw it.

This was a perversion of the bond between human and orc, but it was still there. She needed, he gave, over and over. I watched her realise that she couldn't rely on that anymore, that he couldn't give her this help, even though he'd brought her all this way. I pushed my way through my mates to the sounds of their grumbles, but for all their protectiveness, they knew that sometimes there were things I needed to do. I went and took Mahk's hands in mine.

"What're you doing, honey? He can't come where we're going. None of them can. I get you've bonded and whatnot…"

I let her selfish dribble drop away as I stared up at the orc. His plaits had grey threaded through them and there were lines on his face, but he was still a strong warrior, a vital one. So I leant forward, and on automatic, he did the same, knowing the ritual better than me. Our foreheads pressed together.

Can you hear me, Mothers? It's me, Laila. I've never really prayed to you before, I thought. *I don't even know if you do that, are receptive to that.* My teeth found my bottom lip. *But one of your loyal and faithful sons, he's here and he's about to get his fucking heart broken. He's either going to let Susie go.* I saw the flames inside him stutter at that thought. *Or he's going to come with her.*

That would be the worst option, I realised. Like, I knew that before, but just how awful it would be hit me hard. Being left adrift in a realm, a world, where he had no one that cared for him, as Susie went swanning back to the US, where what he was would have to be hidden, masked, kept contained. I reached for his hands, feeling them limp and unresponsive in mine as I gave them a squeeze.

Please, Mothers. If you have some kind of divine plan, some sort of matchmaking operation from the heavens, let Mahk find the one he deserves. Don't let it go down like this. Don't let him die with his heart breaking for a woman that never cared for him.

I can't exactly tell you what happened afterwards. I went perfectly still, and so did Mahk, I remember that. Something flared bright, then brighter still, inside us, and then…

"Lay-la?" Ghain asked, having appeared at my shoulder.

Mahk jerked away from me, a light flaring in his eyes that I didn't understand, but he just stared as if seeing us for the first time. The fire inside him, it flickered warily, building up to something, but… He raised a hand to Susie, who didn't see this farewell as she was too busy berating, then pleading with my mates in turns, but they did. They raised their hands to Mahk, a salute to him, to his endurance, to his attempts to keep the Mothers' grace alive, despite the challenges he'd faced. Then he pulled his axe from his back and took off, running into the darkness and towards her…

"You guys ready?" Bruce asked, sticking his head through the portal.

Susie answered, loudly and insistently, but Bruce just glared at her, shutting her up finally.

"My mate?" Vargan asked, one last time, and I nodded, walking towards them and through the place between.

Chapter 29

This was the end of my story, my HEA. Well, almost. There were a few things I needed to take care of still...

"They keep hassling me about meeting my parents," I said to Hannah as we walked up Monster Street, passing shops and waving to people we knew. The neighbourhood was definitely a friendly one, with multiple families coming by to welcome us, bringing housewarming gifts and hanging around for a coffee. "For them, it's the last step. Well, before y'know..."

"Babies?" she said with a broad grin. "Cute little chubby cheeked orc babies!"

"Yeah, that. I'm holding off telling Mum and Dad because their heads will explode, but also..."

"Also, you're not ready to be a mother?" she said more gently. "They know that. It's probably why they're so focussed on meeting your parents." She stopped and smiled at me. "They think it will help you to get ready."

"But...how do I do it? How do you introduce two humans to this?" I waved my hands at the elves who were chatting with the dryad florist, the tree spirit encouraging their potted fruit trees to produce more and more fruit.

"Let's get this done first, then we'll sit down and brainstorm it," Hannah said, nodding to the jewellery shop behind us. "It's not an easy process, that's for sure."

"I know," I said, pulling out a Ziplock bag from my purse. "They think if they get Dad a bottle of OP rum and Mum a box of chocolates, all will be well." I let out a long sigh. "Probably because it was with Judith, Vargan's mum. She was just like cool, this is how mating an orc goes."

I scrubbed my fingers along my scalp, then walked up to the jewellers' shop and opened the door.

"YES," Draco said, looking up from a piece he was working on, a gilt jewellery loupe in one eye. But when he removed it, he frowned. "You are the girls that do not wish to spend money on jewellery. I have no time for you."

"No, then you wouldn't be interested in these?" I said idly, tossing the bag on the counter. There were several precious stones and some ores as well.

Like a shark sensing blood in the water, the dragon shifter's eyes fluttered, changing to a golden yellow with a snakelike vertical pupil. His fingers snatched the bag up, tearing the thin plastic to get to the stones. He held up one, then another to the light, then frowned down at me.

"Where did you get these from?" he asked me.

Be careful, very careful, Lily had told me. The Chinese dragon shifter had given me some tips for this negotiation, as apparently, her kind wasn't quite so motivated by wealth as European dragons were.

"Lunor," I replied.

"Hello, ladies," Frag said as he emerged from the back. "And how are you—"

"You need to buy these. Now," Draco insisted. "Give them whatever they want for them. They are very fine quality, especially for their size. Exceptional."

"There goes our bargaining chip…" Frag hissed and then

came over, leaning on the glass display case, his eyes beginning to gleam as we started to bargain.

I GOT MORE than just money that day. Draco was very keen to buy any other stones or ores we might have and gave us a damn good price for them. The orcs were definite about us staying together, being 'co-dependant,' and now we had the means to do so. It was as we were concluding the first transaction, a sizeable chunk of money going into our accounts, when I saw him.

I don't know why I looked up, the banter between Draco and Frag seeming to fall away as I watched him walk past. The same dashing good looks, the same sandy hair swept back from his face, the same beard. I heard Hannah say something to me, but it was all quiet and muffled. I swung out the jewellery shop door and onto the street, weaving past the few people walking by until I drew up beside him. He turned to glance at me, surely wondering who this random chick was, but when I persisted on staring, he stopped.

"You," I said, pointing a finger at him.

"Me?" He had the same demeanour, slightly irritated by everything. "Can I help you…?"

"You already did," I snapped back, Hannah running up to stand beside me. "You sent me into the orc realm."

"The orc…?" He frowned, then peered more closely at me, a slow smile spreading across his face. "That's how it turned out? You're the girl with the fae friend at Ingress, though obviously, you worked out finally that she wasn't human." He looked Hannah's fluttering wings over with a quick glance.

"What did you do?" I asked in a low growl. "What did you do to Susie in 1969?"

"What did I do? I gave you a Heart's Desire potion, and for free, thank you very much. Usually, I ask for a first-born child or something, but…" He looked at me, then Hannah. "You looked bloody miserable but were trying so hard not to be. You could've been mean, jealous of your fae friend's glamour and the way she lured in human men, but you weren't."

He shrugged.

"I pour drinks there some nights for a friend and was feeling somewhat jaded by human behaviour, what with all the gym bros acting like douches, when you walked in. I thought fuck it, let's see what comes of this, and made you a glass of Heart's Desire. So did you find what you wanted most in the world?"

I stopped then, not looking at this random guy or the street or even Hannah, feeling the flicker of the fire inside me burn brighter.

"Yeah…" I said. "I think I did. I mean, not everything." I frowned slightly. "It causes as many problems as it solves them. The one you gave Susie in 1969 made people incredibly unhappy. My orc mates want to meet my parents and I've got no idea how to make that work…"

"It can," he said with a snort. "It depends on what kind of heart you have. And this Susie, in 1969? I gotta admit, I don't remember too much of the sixties, if you take my drift." He winked at us. "But if you've got problems, it's just because you haven't worked out exactly what you desire yet. The potion doesn't fade away. You'll be one of the lucky ones your whole life, if you can just work out what you want. It doesn't work if you don't. Magic is all about intent."

"What?" I said, blinking. "So all I have to do is wish—"

"I'm a wizard, not a genie," he replied with a snort. "You have to desire it with all of your heart." He reached across, tapping my breastbone, and when he did, that same fire burned so much hotter. "Look into your heart and find what you really, really want. If your heart is true, you'll find happiness. If it's not…"

I thought of Susie and her myopic focus, entirely centred on herself. She'd just as likely desired to be worshipped, but when she was by orcs who would do anything for her, she'd spurned it as not good enough. But me…? I frowned slightly, knew Hannah was chatting to the man, but not really hearing it.

I could only hear something else.

I turned on my heel, striding down the street, weaving between people, finding them without even trying in the local supermarket, picking us up supplies.

"How did the negotiations go with the dragon, my mate?" Vargan asked.

"Do we need to sever the lowly serpent's throat for disrespecting you?" Kren asked, peering at me.

"We need to get the gifts," I said.

"What gifts, my Lay-la?" Ghain asked, but the others knew. They dumped the bags of groceries on Ghain and then disappeared back into the shops to purchase gifts for my parents.

AND SO, once we got home, everything came full circle. Hannah was sitting on the couch, my mates clustered around me as I opened my sketchbook to a fresh page. My fingers hovered over pens and textas, selecting them at random as I began to draw.

I didn't really do comics. I wasn't much of a storyteller, but now I needed to be. My eyes and heart burned as I drew the outside of the house, a strange car pulling up, then two people got out. They looked around themselves in wonder and then went and knocked on the door. The sound of it, here and now, made everyone jump, and then Hannah frowned as she got to her feet, going and answering it. I drew Mum and Dad there, looking quizzical, seeing my best friend in her true form, their mouths dropping open at the sight of her wings.

But in the next frame, their faces softened. They made a fuss of how beautiful they were, how beautiful she always was, and then they gave her a hug.

"We were just out for a drive and…"

My orcs were on their feet the minute my parents stepped in and my pen hung between my fingers as Mum and Dad stared at my mates and my mates stared back.

"Laila?" Dad said, a question in his voice.

"Dad, Mum." I stood up as well. "This is Vargan, Kren, and Ghain. They are my mates."

"Mates…" Mum breathed the word. "They're…?"

"My husbands, I guess. I wanted to tell you, to let you know, but…"

"No, no, love. I can see why."

My parents edged closer, just staring and staring as their minds fought to take this all in, when something occurred to me. I went closer, moving slowly, then reached out and gave my mum a hug.

The Mothers' grace, that fire that burned within us, it was love, of course. So while my parents might never have known a sky with three moons, they did know that. They loved me, rather desperately it appeared, as it all came rushing in. Their fears, their worries, their concerns, and now? Their complete and utter shock.

"They love me," I told Mum, letting her see that fire that burned inside me now. "They'll always protect me," I told Dad.

"Always, Dennis, son of Trevor," Vargan said, putting his hand on his chest, then holding out his palm. "And we have gifts to demonstrate our worthiness." Kren passed him the bottle of rum and Vargan had to close Dad's fingers around the box when he offered it, my parents still staring blankly at them.

"For you, Tray-cee, daughter of Lois," Ghain said, doing the same with the massive box of chocolates they had bought.

And for a moment, maybe more than one, there was only silence as we watched and waited, to see how they would respond.

"YOU'RE...MARRIED?" Mum asked.

"Well, not officially," I replied, my mates growling at that. "But in every way that matters."

"Oh my god, Laila!" she said finally, clapping her hands to her face as happy tears sprung up, her smile radiant. "I'm finally going to get grandkids!"

"When Lay-la is ready, she tells us," Vargan said, a slow smile spreading across his face.

"Ready? Ready! Laila, you're not getting any younger, you know. And look at these big strapping boys! You can't…"

I let her frenzied words wash over me, watched my mates talk to my parents, planning out allll the children I was apparently going to have, when Hannah sidled over.

"Heart's Desire, huh?" she asked. "Looks like it's working out all right so far."

"Almost," I said. "There's just one more thing."

LATER, much later, after the guys had cooked a truly horrifying BBQ lunch. After we'd sat down to eat it, the guys crunching the ill cooked meal with gusto. After the long protracted leave taking that happens at the end of a family get together. After Hannah left too, with a hug and promise to do lunch, I went back outside, sitting down on the patio with my art supplies and my sketchbook.

"That went well," Kren said in a decisive tone. "Dennis told us embarrassing stories from our mate's childhood, and we charred the meat of your people according to your customs."

"And Tray-cee seems to approve of the idea of children greatly," Ghain said with a sly look my way.

"Our mate tricked the dragon shifter into giving us much gold for the stones of our people," Vargan said. "We are safe, secure, and happy in our territory."

"There's just one more thing…" I said under my breath, looking out over the backyard, sketching in the grass, the bushes, and the trees, then something else.

Their eyes jerked sideways as they saw the flare of light, as a small, stable rift in reality formed. Away from humans, away from anyone who would get hurt, but a means for my loves and my future sons to be able to walk freely in both worlds.

"One more thing?" Kren said.

Their groans filled the air, but that wasn't the only sound. As

I got to my feet, as they came with me, tracking me as surely as a painted cat did its prey, I heard the drums in my ears. I looked up, seeing that the moon had begun to rise, but as we walked into the trees, searching for the place in between, they fell away and were replaced by walls of rock.

"Well, that didn't take long at all," Judith said with a smile.

What's next?

Looking for monsters goodness? Fighting Monsters will be about 200k of kraken, satyr, gargoyle and minotaur goodness! Two books, release simultaneously for bingey good times!

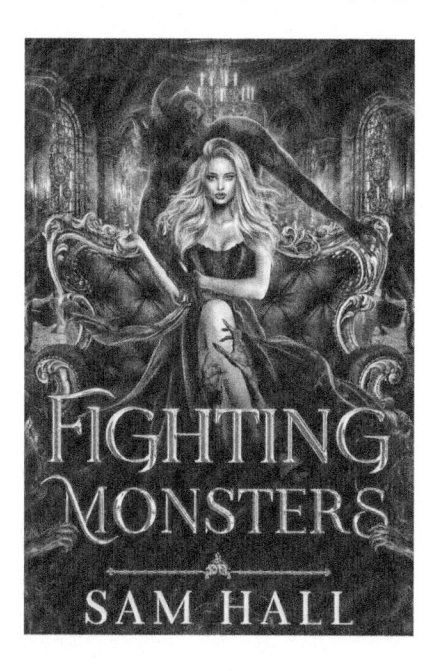

What's next?

Get it here

Acknowledgments

Super editor Meghan Leigh Daigle worked like a Trojan on this one! Thank you so much for getting this one done at a difficult time.
   https://www.facebook.com/Bookish-Dreams-Editing-105567517555119/

Cover was created by the team at Gombar Cover Designs

Special thanks to Mollie, Cherie, Kayla, Dianne, Jessie, Joanne, Richelle, Steph, Lizzy and Renee. This was a crazy ride and you came along with me on it!

About the Author

I grew up in that bit of Australia you saw in Crocodile Dundee. Yup, I have seen saltwater crocs in the wild, have held a koala (the 70s, when stressing wildlife for the kiddies was still cool) and have swatted an insane number of hand sized spiders (they think I am their queen and are always wherever I am!). I have a gorgeous child with ASD, a super supportive, truly awesome partner and so, so many animals. Seriously, there are double the pets to people.

Being a little baby writer, trying to make her way in the big, crowded, world of self-publishing, reviews are our lifeblood. Seriously, we're sitting in isolated rooms wondering what the hell we are doing with our lives, so chuck a review on Amazon or Goodreads and I will loooove you!

Printed in Great Britain
by Amazon